Down Dog
Diary

Also by
SHERRY ROBERTS

Book of Mercy
Maud's House
WriteTips

Down Dog
Diary

A Novel by
SHERRY ROBERTS

Osmyrrah Publishing | Apple Valley, Minnesota

Osmyrrah Publishing
Apple Valley, Minnesota 55124
www.osmyrrahpublishing.com
info@osmyrrahpublishing.com

ISBN: 978-0-9638880-7-5

Printed in the United States of America
First Edition

Cover Digital Art by Kathey Amaral: designbykatt.deviantart.com
Photography by Cathleen Tarawhiti: www.facebook.com/pages/
Cathleen-Tarawhiti-Photographer/95878166172
Model: Monique Wanner

TO TONY, WHO KEEPS ME GROUNDED
BUT ALSO INSISTS THAT I FLY.

THE DREAM ENDS

JAMES TUMBLETHORNE, KNOWN AS "Tum," was not an easy man to kill.

On a crisp February morning with the haze still embracing the hills outside Taos, he woke exhausted, tied to a wooden kitchen chair. He remembered the knock on the door and then the jolts. Lifting his head, his long gray hair in his eyes, he saw he was not alone.

The two men, same white blond buzz cuts, same big shoulders squeezed into boxy silk suits, looked eerily alike. One flipped open a switchblade, stabbed the couch cushion, and ripped it open. The other swept cereal and canned goods from the kitchen cabinets and dumped bags of flour, filling the air with white powder.

In Tum's small adobe home, there was little room for

chaos—either physically or spiritually. It was just two rooms, the kitchen/living area currently being demolished and the bedroom. He always kept his home tidy and calm. He had built this refuge with his own hands, hauled the oven up on a sled behind his Harley, made the windows intentionally large to welcome the peace of the mountain. And now the peace was gone.

Suit One in the living room was frustrated; he heaved Tum's sacred drum against the wall and kicked over the coffee table, scattering stones and feathers across the Navajo rug. Suit Two, in the kitchen, flipped through Tum's Killer Sudoku book then ripped it in two with a growl. Tum heard the crunch of pottery, saw it was his favorite bread-making bowl, and swore. He pulled at the plastic restraints that bound his arms behind his back.

Tum had been Tasered before. There's no forgetting the unbearable pain that hijacks the central nervous system. Fifty thousand volts passing through the human body is not pleasant—muscles lock, body slams to the floor, and afterward, the muscles tingle and twitch like a fish on a dock. Tum had never passed out before from being stunned, so someone must have clobbered him when he was down. His head ached.

There were grown bears smaller than James Tumblethorne. He was not a helpless man. His tattooed bulk sported numerous souvenirs from sharp knives, broken bottles, splintered chairs, brass knuckles. That was before he found peace in the mountains and high deserts of New Mexico, before he became one with Spirit. Before he began to follow his calling to become a shaman.

Tum tugged again at the plastic handcuffs. No feather-weight, he still pumped iron at the age of seventy-two; his zapped deadweight body must have been a bitch to drag up from the floor and position in a chair. The thought made him smile. He hoped the bastards got hernias.

Suit One, the guy handy with the Taser, ripped a dream catcher from the wall and tossed it aside. He leaned over Tum, shouting, "Where is it, you crazy old man? Where is it?" Tum could smell him, frustration mixed with some fancy cologne. It made him want to sneeze.

The Suit paced behind him, gulping deep breaths, trying to calm himself. Tum sure as hell didn't want to go out at the hands of a Suit. He always thought the end would come as he sat in his ceremonial kiva, praying to Spirit. He'd imagined his body old and tired from this journey but his spirit happy and calm. He'd imagined Great Spirit lifting him on the wings of a circling crow. He did not want to be delivered to Spirit in the claws of a vulture.

The man circled the chair and came to a stop in front of Tum. "The shaman's book. I want it. Now."

Crashes from the bedroom. More ripping sounds. There went his mattress. Tum sniffed the air and glanced at the oven. His sourdough bread was burning. He loved making bread, working the dough with his big hands. It was a peace-ful activity. And these guys were ruining it.

The men had neglected to tie his feet, a mistake he could work with. He might just get out of this after all. When the Suit leaned into Tum's face again, Tum kicked out, sweep-ing the man's legs out from under him. The Suit tumbled to the floor. With a roar and an explosion of energy, Tum splintered the chair spindle he was tied to, powered himself to his feet, and aimed a kick at the man's head. But the man was quicker than Tum expected. The Suit recovered, grabbed Tum's boot, and twisted it. No hands free to catch himself, Tum crashed to the floor like a falling tree. The Suit jammed the Taser into Tum's chest. Two jolts left him gasping. Weakness flooded his body.

The Suit sneered at him, "Think you can take me, old man?"

The Suit was on his feet now, looking down at Tum. He aimed a kick at Tum's ribs. Tum tried to roll away, but his body didn't respond. The Suit called for his partner, and they pulled another kitchen chair into the center of the room, hauled Tum up, and wrestled him into it. Pain shot through him; one rib, maybe two, broken.

Outside, the crows were becoming unhinged. Something was wrong in the world, and they knew it. One flew against the window making the Suit jump. He nodded toward the door and said to his partner, "Shoot those fucking birds." No, screamed Tum in his head. Suit Two went outside. Shots split the air. Wings scattered. More shots. Tum closed his eyes.

When he'd left the wild life, Tum needed to be near goodness and light. At the Whispering Spirit Farm, which still stood not far from here as the crow flies over the mountain, he'd found these and had been reborn. He'd found them working in the garden, the kitchen, the barn. Taking care of the children. How he loved the children. His friend Nico said he must have been a nanny in another life. He'd been a part of the community for two years when Great Spirit called.

On the day he received the calling, he was hunkered down with his bike under a big old oak, a monster thunderstorm squatting above him. Suddenly, the monster's lightning fingers flicked the tree, and electricity raced down the trunk, along the roots, and reached up through Tum's thick black leather boots, flinging him like a doll. When he awoke, he had memories of white light. Did he die or was that just an echo of the lightning's laughter? He felt different, in possession of a new clarity, of an inner knowing. He realized he had been searching for someone to heal him, when the truth was inside him all along. He climbed on his bike, pointing it toward home, to Whispering Spirit Farm. What an amazing ride that had been. He saw connections everywhere—between him and the wind and the trees along the road. He saw the interconnectedness of everything, the power we all have inside us, and—for the first time—he paid attention.

The Suit poked him with the Taser.

Tum opened his eyes slowly and stared at the man. Tum would never let the shaman's book fall into the hands of this SOB. The book, a diary, was passed down from keeper to keeper. A healer in Mexico, on his way to meet Great Spirit, had placed the diary in Tum's hands. Tum had added his own insights and experiences to the book, just as had the shamans before him. But more importantly, the healer had whispered, it was Tum's job now to keep it safe.

The Suit tapped the Taser against his palm. There was a tattoo on the back of the man's left hand—a waste of good ink. A skull chomping down on a flaming heart moved in rhythm with each impatient tap.

Tum refused to talk to this piece of shit. He knew silence

could be unnerving, maddening—a trick he'd used in count-less police interrogation rooms after biker brawls. But these men were not bound by laws and department regulations. Over and over, the Suit with the tattoo sent Taser charges ripping through Tum's body, leaving him gulping for air, more exhausted with each stun. Yet he would not speak. He would not speak of the secrets of the diary, of the lawyer's office where it was locked in a safe, of Maya Skye.

His last will and testament was specific about where his worldly possessions would go, and Nico, his lawyer, knew what to do. They'd shared the road for many years, broth-ers of the leather. Nico would deliver the diary to its new keeper, to Tum's unlucky heir.

Tum looked up and saw the Suit had a gun now. It was aimed at Tum's forehead.

"Last chance to talk," the man snarled. "No? Well, you big bastard, think on this: I'll get to your friends, your neighbors, your relatives. I'll find them. Somebody has that book."

Tum closed his eyes and sent one final prayer: *Spirit, pro-tect her.*

And then James Tumblethorne heard the last words he would ever hear on this earth: "Have it your way, you old fucker. Peace out!"

CHAPTER 1

CORPSE POSE

IN THE QUIET OF my kitchen, I slid the letter from its envelope. Sadness still rose in my throat, even though I'd read it many times. The letter began, "If you're reading this, kid, I'm wiggling up the cosmic stream like some fat old tattooed salmon. Sorry to leave you with a mess . . ."

That was the way my old nanny, James Tumblethorne, said good-bye.

Tum roared into my life when I was four, a bigger-than-life man on a huge, noisy machine. He had barely booted the kickstand of his motorcycle into place before he swept me into the air and asked me my name. Our connection had been that instant—he knew it was right to snap me up, and I knew it was right to trust this wild stranger. And now he

7

had left me, the daughter he never had, the one he'd guided and loved like no other.

The hole in my life was big enough to drive his Harley through.

Sniffing, not bothering to wipe the tears from my cheeks, I smoothed the paper Tum had touched, my fingers tracing its amazingly lovely penmanship. Where had a man who was more likely to use his hands to break a jaw than push a pen learned such graceful loops and elegant swishes? I loved the way he made the "y" with a flourish, as if my name deserved special care.

I am Maya Skye. I am named for a civilization that tracked celestial bodies without telescopes or computers, that built enormous and beautiful architecture, that developed a written language while others were still grunting. But they also cut out the still-beating hearts of young girls to appease spirits, and they decapitated the losing team in sporting events. In some ways, I am very much like the Mayas: I'm a dreamer, a stargazer, but I have a bit of the bloodthirsty in me, too.

This is a problem for one dedicated to enlightenment. I am a yoga teacher. My calling is to help others. I do not take this responsibility lightly, no matter the karmic consequences. It has always been this way.

Whenever I fought with some other kid in the commune, filling Whispering Spirit Farm with all manner of violent vibes, I'd flee my mother's disappointed eyes and seek out Tum. He would lift me onto his massive shoulders and warn in a gruff voice eroded by years of cigarettes and bar smoke: "Kicking ass will catch up with you, kid." He was right.

TUM'S LETTER HAD BEEN tucked inside a book that, frankly, scared the dickens out of me. I knew this book. It was the journal of James Tumblethorne, the shaman's diary.

I remembered the diary being bigger—and more mysterious. The last time I'd seen it I was only nine. That was twenty-six years ago. The book, and I, had been through much since then, and, to be honest, I had come through the years in better shape.

The diary was the repository not only of Tum's wisdom and prayers, but the wisdom and prayers of all those who came before him, people who had followed the shaman's path. Pages were falling out of the well-traveled journal, now held together with a rubber band. Some entries were written in languages I could not decipher. Words were stained with dirt and perhaps blood. The ink ran on pages rippled by raindrops (or were they tears?). The black leather cover was soft with age and worn in spots, and one corner looked as if someone had tried to set it afire.

I brought the diary to my nose, gently riffled the pages, and sniffed. I expected the moldy smell of old paper. Instead, the scent of roses swirled into the air. Then, the aroma changed—to the fresh smell of mint crushed between one's fingertips, to pine forest, to wet dog. I frowned. I flipped the edges of the diary with my thumb again. More sweet scents lifted from the pages but mixed in were the smells of rotten things: dumps and puke and death.

A boxelder bug strolled across the kitchen table, crept up the side of the book, and started the trek across one of the first entries, dated 1892. I gently swept the bug into my cupped palm, took it outside, and dropped it in the snowy bush beside the door. Boxelders are hearty, up to the chill of even a February day in Minnesota.

I returned to Tum's journal, closed my eyes, and opened the book to a random page. The smell of axle grease greeted me. I opened my eyes and immediately recognized Tum's looping handwriting. It made me smile, like an old friend welcoming me. It said:

I have traveled many roads. They are all inside me, sometimes tangling with each other, sometimes living in peace, sometimes just ignoring each other. They are me, but I am not them. With the twist of a thought, I turn them into strings of yarn . . .

I felt a surge of power snaking up through my fingers, streaking up my arm.

I slammed the book shut.

It was said the shaman's diary held mysteries not meant for ordinary men and women. And now these secrets sat on my kitchen table.

WHEN THE MONDAY AFTERNOON yoga class began to arrive downstairs, I stashed the diary in my desk, which was old and no longer locked. Some of its wooden drawers were swollen with age and complained when I pulled them open. My new role of protector of the shaman's diary weighed heavily on me. The desk did not inspire confidence. Obviously, I needed better security, maybe something along the lines of Fort Knox. I was not just being paranoid. Ever since a lawyer named Nico delivered the diary five days ago, there had been something amiss in my home, something ominous in the air. I have always been sensitive to energies, both good and foreboding. It sure felt as if I had some bad vibes on my hands now. I itched with an urgent need to fix this situation, to cleanse the remodeled fire station where I live and teach. I own Breathe, the only yoga studio in Gabriel's Garden, Minnesota.

I guess I like the Monday class because it happens to be full of grouches and nonbelievers and people who would rather be somewhere else, like the new guy, who looks great from behind in Downward Facing Dog. Down Dog is a pose that turns you upside down, gives you a new perspective, strengthens you. What's not to like about it? You hang out, bent like an inverted V or a leggy Afghan hound stretching after a wonderful nap, pushing into the floor with strong arms and legs. I tell my students to use this pose to rest and regain energy, and to do it whenever they feel like it. The new guy, Peter Jorn, feels like it a lot.

Jorn showed up two weeks ago, and the first thing he said to me was, "I don't believe in this yoga stuff."

I handed him a punch card good for twelve classes and said, "*Namaste*, Oh Honorable Skeptic." *Namaste* is sort of a yogic aloha that means the divine in me honors the divine in you. I believe there is the divine in everyone. Just sometimes you have to go through a lot of mud and muck to get to it. That's what yoga does. It burrows a path.

Jorn is something of a burrower himself. He digs for stories. As a journalist, he's big on facts and the truth but a bit vague on his personal life. I only know that he inherited the town newspaper, *The Independent,* when his uncle moved to Florida, and that he's recovering from multiple gunshot wounds. He prefers to keep it all hush-hush, but I've seen the way he rubs the scar at his temple and how he favors his right shoulder and hip.

The yoga studio is a large room that once housed Gabriel's Garden's single fire truck. During class, I roam through the room, quietly moving among my students, stopping beside mats spread across the oak floor, adjusting an arm here and a leg there.

Today, as usual, I had to remind Alice Dunkirk to breathe. A fit woman in her sixties, Alice marches to Mass every Wednesday and Sunday, rain or shine, climbing over snowbanks or batting away mosquitoes. Every time I get Alice to relax, Catholic guilt winds her up again like a spring.

I placed a calming hand on Olivia's jiggling leg. Olivia Chen, fifteen, petite, with anime eyes, looked at me through her Down Dog legs and wiggled the ring in her left eyebrow. This week her long, bluntly cut black hair had blue streaks.

Before class, I had dimmed the lights and raised the temperature. Sweat glistened on Jorn's arms and dripped from his chin. From the grimace on his face, I could tell his bum shoulder was on fire, and his hip was probably whispering nasty things to him. He'd pushed too hard, again. That's what he did, and he expected his body to respond, to wear down under his insistence and give him what he wanted. Doctors and physical therapists had sent Jorn to yoga, but I knew the Universe had other plans. In yoga, you learn to wait and let answers unfold on their timetable, not yours.

I instructed my students to drop to their knees, roll to their backs, and stretch out their legs. "Relax from the top of your head to the tip of your toes. Melt into the floor. Sink deeper with each breath. This is Corpse Pose."

"I'll say it is," groaned Merlin Huus, the retired carpenter. "I think I'm dead."

There was a collective sigh from the group. I watched my students give in to this restorative pose, all except Jorn. I crouched beside him. "Jorn, you're not relaxing," I whispered in his ear. Jorn's eyes shot open.

"Stop sneaking up on me," he said.

I placed my palm gently on his sore right shoulder and steadily pushed down. He resisted briefly, then sighed. I could feel the shoulder begin to heat under my hand. "Relax. Release. Close your eyes and don't think, Jorn."

Normally, I end class with three *oms* and a *namaste*. But there is power in numbers, and I had those diary vibes to get rid of, so I suggested a variation of a cleansing ceremony I had attended in New Mexico when I was a child. Every year the people of Whispering Spirit Farm piled into vans and onto motorcycles and made the seventy-mile trek south to feed Zozobra at a fiesta in Santa Fe.

Zozobra, or Old Man Gloom, represented the troubles and demons of the past year. It was a giant frowning doll, with flailing arms and a flapping chin. We put our worries, troubles, or fears on scraps of paper and stuffed them into Gloom Boxes. Zozobra devoured the Gloom Boxes and then was set on fire. As he was consumed in flames, we danced in the light of our renewal.

I gathered the class in a circle around my mat. In the

middle of the circle, I'd placed a copper prayer bowl, pens, and paper. I told the class about Old Man Gloom and the tradition we had in our family of not only releasing that which is weighing us down but also inviting the positive to take the place of our troubles and lift us. "So, in our ceremony today, send the prayer that feels right to you," I said. "Write down the trouble you want to go away or the wish or positive thing you want to draw into your life. Place it in the bowl. And we'll burn those suckers."

"I'm not going to get in trouble with the pope for this, am I?" asked Alice.

"It's an ecumenical prayer bowl," I assured her.

Merlin, with enough arthritis for two people, a gift from years of crawling over roofs and pounding hammers, eyed the bowl with suspicion. "I just come to yoga for the fitness."

"Cool," I said. "There's no pressure, Merlin."

Fidgeting Olivia was intrigued. "What happens to the thoughts you put in the bowl? Like where do they go?"

"The spirits will gather them up as smoke and take them where they need to go," I said.

"Spirits. Ha," Peter Jorn muttered.

Merlin sighed and began scribbling on a piece of paper. "I promised my daughter I'd give this yoga thing a chance. I suppose you'd rat me out if I didn't participate."

"In a heartbeat," I smiled.

"I'm in," he said, tossing his paper into the bowl.

Alice wrote something down, folded the paper, then shook her head. She unfolded the paper, scratched out what she had written, and wrote something new. She did this three times before asking, "No one's ever going to see what we wrote, are they?"

"What kind of deep, dark secret are you putting in there, Alice?" teased Julia Lune in a gauzy, floral Southern accent. Julia loved the deep and the dark. Our local celebrity, a romance writer, Julia often had a pen stuck in her disheveled Gibson girl do and joked that she was an expert on passion—not only was she of fiery Russian descent but she was married to a hot Frenchman.

I reassured Alice, "We'll burn them right here and now. Your secrets are safe."

Peter Jorn huffed.

"Well, I think there *are* mysterious things," Olivia said, tossing back her hair and revealing a row of piercings along her ear. "Plus I can use all the help I can get." Olivia's wealthy parents used yoga as after-school care. Olivia was going through a klepto phase. She carefully placed her paper in the bowl, then palmed my pen and stuck it in her pocket.

Julia let her paper flutter down into the bowl, saying, "Well, I never win anything."

By the time Alice was finished with hers, it was folded to the size of a postage stamp. As she gave up her paper to the bowl, she mumbled something about "going to confession."

That left my brother-in-law, David Simpson, and Peter Jorn. We all turned to them.

I knew David was uncomfortable. He'd had to deal with a lot of new thinking since marrying my sister, Heart. Our ways probably seemed foreign to a Minnesota altar boy, high school football star, and the owner of a local landscaping business. Finally, David gave me a look, scribbled something down, and flipped the paper into the bowl. "To keep peace in the family," he said.

Jorn looked around the class. He might not like it, but he knew the value of fitting in—when you interviewed the president of the United States, you didn't do it in desert fatigues and smelling of camel; and when you were sitting around a mountain campfire surrounded by gun-toting guerrillas, you didn't wear a suit and refuse to eat the mystery meat in the cup they shoved in your hand.

"I don't believe in this stuff," he said, as he crinkled his paper into a ball and swished it into the bowl.

I lit a bundle of sage. The earthy smell filled the room and immediately soothed me. As I was about to wave the sage over the bowl, Jorn said, "What about you? You didn't put your paper in. Don't you believe in your own nonsense?"

I had been sending out so many positive vibes to compensate for Jorn's negative ones that I had forgotten the original purpose of all this. I quickly dashed off a few words and added my wish to the others.

The ceremony was short. Waving the sage over the bowl of blazing papers, I led the group in a chant. The smoke from the burning notes rose as it mixed with the smoke of the burning sage. Jorn and Alice refused to chant—Alice for religious reasons and Jorn because of contrariness. But that didn't matter. I felt a shift in the room. Shoulders I hadn't even realized I'd tensed began to relax. I closed my eyes, took a deep breath, and could almost imagine I was back bumping along in the backseat, heading home from Santa Fe, secure in the belief that Zozobra had taken all the gloom away. Peace stole over me. Maybe my fear was unwarranted. Maybe Tum's diary wouldn't suck me down the rabbit hole.

THAT NIGHT I CALLED my sister and told her about Tum. Heart and I are like dark and light. I'm a brunette, and she's a blonde. I love to travel, while she is happiest staying at home. I gaze at the stars, opening my soul to magic, while Heart has found all she needs firmly planted on the ground.

"I'm sorry, Maya," she said. "Tum was weird, but nice."

"I can't believe he's gone," I said. "I assumed he'd always be there, if I needed him, you know?"

"Tum was a big teddy bear. In a nightmarishly tattooed, Hell's Angel sort of way. You were always his favorite."

"Heart?" Knowing how my sister hated remembering our unorthodox childhood in the commune, I fumbled with my thoughts.

"What?"

There was nothing to do but just spit it out. "Tum left me the Down Dog Diary."

There was a pause.

"That son of a bitch," said my sister who never swears.

CHAPTER 2

A TREE
WITH CABIN FEVER

W E KIDS WERE THE ones who began calling it the Down Dog Diary. Yoga classes at Whispering Spirit started when we were young, and one of our favorite poses was Downward Facing Dog. The world looked different in Down Dog, hanging upside down, rear in the air. We all believed the diary had great powers, powers to change anything or anyone, to change the world, like Down Dog. Otherwise, why was it such a big secret? Why did Tum keep it locked in a trunk? No one locked anything at Whispering Spirit.

Since the diary had come back into my life, sleep had been elusive. Memories of Whispering Spirit, my old nanny, and the diary tumbled over each other, revving up my REM state. I had not visited the commune in years, and the last time I saw Tum was six months ago. Finally, I'd had enough. It was 3:30 in the morning, a little over a week since we lit the sage and drove out the bad energies. Wrapped in a big alpaca sweater over leggings, I padded across the cold kitchen floor. I went straight to my desk, pulled open the squeaky drawer, and lifted out the diary.

Swaddling the book in one of my favorite paisley scarves, I whispered a prayer for safekeeping. Then I ran down the spiral stairs that connected my second-floor apartment to the studio on the first floor. Without turning on a light, I passed through Breathe's foyer/office and into the silent yoga studio.

I crossed the large, dark room, the only light coming from the outside lamp by the back door. Buddha smiled from a long, low table against one wall of the studio. Behind him were three loose bricks. I wiggled one brick out and then another, revealing a little cavity in the wall, room enough for something precious. I carefully placed the diary inside, gently tucking the scarf's blue fringe around the book. Then I replaced the bricks, scooted the table back in its old position, and breathed a sigh of relief. I tickled the Hotei Buddha, a chubby fellow, always smiling and content, even though all his worldly possessions fit in a cloth sack. Rubbing the happy Buddha's belly was supposed to bring good fortune.

Darkness pressed against the tall arched windows of the fire station. In the lamplight by the back door, snowflakes swirled in the air. I lit some candles, stepped onto my mat, and began to move in Sun Salutation, welcoming the energy of the sun into my life. And soon I was warm. Without even thinking, I transitioned from yoga into tai chi. Tai chi is moving meditation, a martial art practiced by old ladies in the park and fighters in the ring. It can be used for self-defense or for self-help to bring inner calm, energy, and balance. I had used it for both. In the dark of early morning or late night, in times of stress, I instinctively sought to balance my chi or life energy. My mind calmed as I moved slowly through the forms Tum had taught me, gathering the energy into me, feeling it flow between my hands.

THE PHONE RANG AT 8:15 A.M.

"Maya, get over here. Now."

I knew better than to fool around when my sister used that tone of voice. I tugged on boots and a long down coat, wrapped a purple wool scarf two times around my neck, and scrambled out the door. I forgot my gloves but didn't dare go back for them.

Gabriel's Garden, a little less than an hour's drive northwest of the Twin Cities, straddled prairie and more prairie. It was the kind of place where you chose to raise your children. People moved to Gabriel's Garden because things didn't happen here. They were close enough to the action in the Twin Cities—the restaurants, the touring Broadway shows, the concerts and museums. But not too close. Audio books and snow blowers were popular Christmas gifts in our town of commuters.

I'm sure my parents chose Gabriel's Garden because it sounded like some kind of Eden. They say they feel a sacredness here. And maybe there is. The land was once farmed by the Amish, who worked prayer and a simple life into the dark soil like hands kneading bread dough. My parents taught us that those who traveled before us left their spiritual mark on a place.

The Skye family had certainly left its mark on Gabriel's Garden. My mom and dad migrated here fifteen years ago, bringing with them the family software business, The Skyes the Limit. They had already made a fortune in video gaming with their hit games: Spirit Snatchers and Peace Hero. My sister, Heart, who is manager of the family business, fell in love with David Simpson, a local landscape designer. I opened the town's first yoga studio. And then my geeky millionaire dad, Larry, decided to give a computer to every household in this town of 1,329. Gabriel's Garden went from a sleepy village to "tech town" overnight. The media loved us.

As my Subaru wagon crunched to a halt on the snow-packed road in front of Heart's house, I saw the problem. There were a dozen people gathered on the sidewalk, crowded against the waist-high hedges framing Heart's yard. All faces were turned up to the intense blue sky and to the pink blooms bursting from the black cherry tree in the front yard. Pink in a winter landscape of endless white and gray was a Minnesota miracle.

Heart, on the lookout for me at the front door, hurried through a shoveled opening in the bumper-high snowbank and dragged me toward the house.

Inside, sitting around Heart's weathered kitchen table, were my parents and David, his head clutched in his hands. Heart and David lived in a farmhouse that had been in David's family for generations. Heart loved this house, its history, its big country kitchen, even the constant repairs that David complained about. This home screamed "family" from the pile of boots drying near the wood stove in the corner to crayon drawings on the fridge and the dishes, books, and plants covering every surface of the kitchen counter. Here was the dichotomy of Heart: she wanted the mess of a wholesome family *and* the lovely security of order. While our mother, Evie, effortlessly instilled calm in her surroundings, Heart wrestled her world into serene submission. Look in any drawer or cupboard. You'll find spices organized alphabetically and crisply ironed stacks of bed sheets. Even Heart's "junk" drawer has seen the business end of my sister's labeler.

As we entered, all eyes turned in my direction.

"I didn't do it," I said.

"My cherry tree is blooming," David exclaimed, "in March!"

"It's pretty," I said.

"It's unnatural," said Heart, pointing at the front door with accusation. "It's supposed to bloom in May. And, it has pink flowers."

"That's bad?"

"This tree produces white flowers, Maya."

"It's a horticultural miracle?" I offered.

"It's the diary," Heart said, hugging her long beige cardigan more tightly around her and crossing her arms. "And you know it."

David lifted his head. "What do you mean?" He turned to my father. "What does she mean?" My parents exchanged worried glances.

Larry and Evie Skye tried not to overwhelm their son-in-law with the facts of their alternative lifestyle. Even after ten years of marriage to Heart, David was still on a need-to-know status. Tossing his graying ponytail over his shoulder, Larry explained about James Tumblethorne's passing and the diary he left me. "The diary passes down from shaman to shaman, and each shaman adds his own magic. It has powers."

"Powers?" David frowned. "You've got to be kidding."

Evie, the hub of calm in our family, patted David's arm. "James seldom discussed the diary, but he often helped people with their problems."

"Problems?" David's brow furrowed even further.

"People naturally turned to James when they were worried or afraid or didn't know what to do. Those who do shamanic work are," Evie paused, "clarifiers. Sometimes, they work with energy; sometimes, they simply ask questions that help you find your own clarity." I noticed that Evie avoided describing shamans as intermediaries between the natural and supernatural world. As I said, we tried to be gentle with David when it came to information.

Heart's shoulders were so tense they nearly touched her earlobes. Discussion of our years at the commune had that effect on Heart. According to my parents, they have met and fallen in love in many lifetimes. I don't know if they've ever done the matrimony thing in any of those lives. In their current trip, even though they have taken the same last name to simplify matters for their children, they've decided again to forego the legalities. This never bothered me, but it drove my sister crazy.

As a child, Heart desperately wanted a traditional life with married parents, school buses, and dance lessons. She even legally changed her name to Jane when she was sixteen. We tried to think of her as Jane, but somehow the name Heart kept sneaking back. Even David called her Heart now: Heart Skye Simpson.

When we played make-believe as kids, I always wanted to be the masked avenger. Heart wanted to be a checkout girl at the grocery store. She ached for the ordinary, for a family where you called the parental units "Mom" and "Dad." Growing up in our community, we had many moms and dads; using first names was just more efficient.

"We called it the Down Dog Diary," Heart said quietly. "Tum never allowed us to see or touch it. It was this mysterious thing he kept locked away. I was terrified of the book. We made up all kinds of crazy stories about it."

I grinned. "Yeah, like if you read the words, lasers would shoot out of the text and burn your eyes right out of their sockets."

Evie laughed.

Heart did not. She said, "Another one was if you dared to open the book, you'd unleash a powerful curse, frogs-falling-from-the-sky stuff."

David stared at his wife. "Surely, you don't believe that."

Heart shrugged and turned to me. "You were the only one who was never afraid."

"I begged Tum to let me see it. It was a big secret, and I was a curious kid. But when I touched it . . ."

Heart's eyes widened. "You touched it?"

"It was warm. Like it was alive."

"Alive?" Heart's hand went to her chest.

"But now it feels different."

"How?" Evie asked.

"It feels familiar yet foreign." I thought of the ever-changing scents. "Uncontrollable somehow."

Evie shook her head. "James would never give you something that would harm you."

I knew she was right. Still . . .

"It spooked me. My first thought was to do a cleansing ceremony. I did one. David was there."

"What?" His head came up.

"Remember, after yoga class we burned the papers containing our worries and/or our wishes? And after everyone left, I got out my smudge stick and did another cleansing throughout the house and studio."

David stared at me, and comprehension dawned. "The ceremony. Oh no."

Heart crossed to the table and knelt by her husband's side. "What did you write?"

David paled. "I was worried about the business. Last year was a tough one. I just wanted to wipe it out and have something 'spectacular' happen."

"Oh, David." Heart slumped back on her heels.

"I didn't know." David looked at his wife in horror, then shook his head. "I don't believe in all this stuff. Cleansing ceremonies, magic diaries, cherry trees that bloom in the dead of winter."

At that moment, Sadie shuffled in, her footie pajamas slapping the linoleum floor. She gave a big yawn and crawled into David's lap, curling up her long, eight-year-old legs.

She dropped her head on his chest and said, "Nice tree, Daddy."

THE CROWD IN THE front yard grew, and it wasn't long before Peter Jorn sniffed out a story and came knocking at the door. I let him in. "I can't wait to hear this one," he said, as if every weird thing he had to report on in Gabriel's Garden was my fault.

Evie welcomed Jorn with a warm smile and offered him some decaf oolong tea. My mother radiates serenity from the tips of her spiky gray hair to the toes of her old-style penny loafers. It is nearly impossible to growl at Evie.

Jorn politely turned down the tea then glanced around the kitchen. I knew immediately he was looking for the coffee pot. "Caffeine tenses up your shoulders," I told him.

Eyeing the heavy mug on the table near David's hand, Jorn replied, "I'll risk it."

Larry, ever the peacemaker, jumped up from the table with his usual energy and poured Jorn a cup of coffee. Nodding his thanks to Larry, Jorn sat down in a chair next to David.

"So what's with the tree?"

"It looks like cotton candy," Sadie said.

Jorn leaned closer to David and lowered his voice. "I'm no expert, but should it be doing that—in March? Is it some weird horticultural experiment?"

Heart objected. "He's a businessman, not some mad scientist."

"Then what's the deal?"

"I honestly don't know!" David said. "Yesterday, it was completely dormant, not a bud in sight, and today it's blooming like springtime on the Washington Freaking Mall."

"David!" Heart rolled her eyes toward Sadie. "Young ears."

"It's okay, Mommy, I didn't freaking hear it."

Heart sighed.

I glanced at Larry, who was deep in thought. While Evie favored simple white button-down blouses and trim slacks, Larry was seldom seen out of flannel, jeans, and tennis shoes and could slip into geekdom before your very eyes. When he got that far-off look, he was working some software issue or geek problem and you might as well come back later. That was one of the reasons he and Evie left Whispering Spirit, the community they had helped found—not enough power outlets for Larry's technology needs.

The instant Larry snapped back from the labyrinthine corridors of his thoughts, his eyes widened, and he cleared his throat. "Maybe we need to be worrying about other ramifications."

"Other ramifications?" Jorn and David asked at the same time.

Larry spread his hands. "We really can't do much about the tree. It is what it is. It's bloomed, and there's nothing we can do about it. We can call it a freak of nature."

Jorn raised an eyebrow. "Why wouldn't we call it a freak a nature? That's what it is, isn't it?"

Ignoring Jorn, Larry turned to me, "Have you checked with your other students?"

I could see where my father was going with this. Larry was worried that other unusual instances from our cleansing ceremony were about to manifest in Gabriel's Garden. I filled Jorn in: on Tum, the diary, and how we suspected that the cherry tree's early blooming was related to the cleansing ceremony, which was related to the shaman's diary that I now owned.

"I don't believe it." Jorn sat back and looked around the group.

I turned to my parents. "I'll fix this," I said.

Evie stood and came to me, placing her hand on my shoulder. "Maya, you don't have to always save the world."

I nodded, but just then, my phone chimed in my pocket. I jumped. It was Mary, Merlin Huus's daughter. "Can you stop by? I've got a problem."

CHAPTER 3

MICHELIN MAN
GETS HIS WISH

M Y PARENTS LOVE TO tell the story of my conception amid the ruins of an ancient culture while the sea crashed against the shore below them. They'd left Heart, who was about two, at home in New Mexico with a multitude of mommies and daddies and hitched a ride to the Mexican Yucatán. It was the autumnal equinox, and there was a helluva party planned at Tulum, the Maya ruins.

Evie always gets that soft, dreamy look when she recounts the event. "The Mayas built their temples to enhance their rituals and human sacrifices. It is deliciously mathematical. On the equinox, the sun's rays shoot through two stone structures built in a keyhole shape. The light is directed across the ceremonial city of Tulum to the entrance. The sea is bashing at the bottom of the cliffs below. The birds are wheeling and calling, the iguanas scampering. The breeze rustles the palms. You can practically breathe the romance. Larry and I made it right in the ruins when the sun was coming up. It was so spiritual. That's why Maya is the creature she is. She was conceived right there in the vortex of centuries of passion and lust. The vibes knocked us off our feet."

I have heard this story many times. The drama of my beginnings is in my soul. Maybe it's why I never see a kung fu movie I don't like or why I'm fascinated by math despite the fact that I can't balance my checkbook. Maybe it was why I followed a scream into a New York alley one night and came out a changed woman.

As I left Heart's house and drove to the home of Merlin's daughter on Elm Street, that old feeling settled on me. If Merlin was in trouble, I had to help. As I got out of my Subaru in front of the Huus house and slammed the door, Peter Jorn pulled up behind me. With his sore hip, he took his time climbing out of his old Jeep.

"What are you doing here?"

"As much as I hate to admit it, this *is* a story. So where you go, I go. We're going to put an end to this diary nonsense so I can go home and hit the Internet for articles on cherry trees. There has to be a logical explanation for this."

I shrugged.

Merlin's granddaughter answered the front doorbell and directed us to the backyard.

"What's Merlin doing? Shoveling?" I asked.

"No, he's bouncing." The girl, about four, began jumping

up and down. "My mom says Grandpa's going to break his neck. As soon as I get my snow pants on, I'm going out to break my neck, too."

We circled the house, crunching through the snow, following a thump thump thump and Merlin's hooting and hollering as he flung his bony seventy-nine-year-old body into the air. He was having the time of his life on his granddaughter's trampoline, which he had cleared of snow with a broom. There were little piles of snow that he'd missed, that shifted with each thump and leaped into the air with Merlin. The trampoline was one of those big round affairs, at least sixteen feet in diameter, with poles supporting net walls to keep the children—and now Merlin—from bouncing out and landing on the family dog. As we rounded the corner of the house, Merlin cried out, "Hot damn, Maya, look at me. I can do a flip. You wanna see?"

Merlin Huus, who'd learned the fine art of cabinetmaking from his Danish father and flips from watching his granddaughter, was bundled up against the March cold in puffy quilted coveralls and brightly striped socks, hat, and scarf. He nursed a constant sore back and stiff joints from a lifetime of bending over and squatting while coaxing life into wood. In the last yoga class, when he bent at the waist, he could barely reach mid-shin with his fingertips. Today he was doing front somersaults on a trampoline like the Michelin man in Cirque du Soleil.

"Awesome, Merlin," I laughed. He was so busy grinning at me he turned a flip into a flop. I held my breath, but he bounced back up all smiles.

"This is ridiculous," Jorn muttered. "His old bones can't take this kind of punishment. Get him out of there."

"Party pooper," I said to Jorn. I turned to Merlin. "Ah, Merlin, can you take a break?"

"I don't know. I wanna practice one of those jumps the Russian fellas do."

"Please, Merlin. It's sort of important."

"Okey-dokey." Merlin bounced to the trampoline door in his stocking feet. He slipped on his boots and jumped to the ground.

In the Huus kitchen, Merlin's daughter Mary hovered, making sure everyone had hot chocolate. She pushed a plate of fresh-baked ginger snaps toward us and cast a worried glance at her father, who, oblivious to us all, was chasing marshmallows in his hot chocolate with a spoon. "Maya, maybe as his yoga teacher and all, you can tell him to cool it on the trampoline?" Mary asked.

"I'll see what I can do."

As Mary bustled her daughter out of the kitchen, I turned to Merlin. Before I could speak, Merlin gushed, "Maya, I feel like a man of forty. No aches, no pains, no creaks. God, it feels so good to just walk, to just move. This yoga is some powerful stuff."

Jorn and I exchanged looks.

"You think it's the yoga, Merlin?" Jorn asked.

"What else can it be? It sure ain't my vitamins." He leaned toward Jorn. "Man, I'm feeling frisky, if you know what I mean?"

I cleared my throat. "Merlin, about your new-found energy, I don't think it's entirely from yoga."

"No?"

"Remember last week when we did the cleansing ceremony after class? What did you write down?"

Merlin didn't hesitate. "Take these old aches away. That's what I wrote. And it came true. I'm tired of feeling old, Maya. I want to feel young again."

"Did this just come on all of a sudden, this new vitality, Merlin?" Jorn asked.

"All week I've been sleepin' damn good, which is, in itself, a miracle," Merlin said. "I usually get up three or four times a night. But lately, I'm sleepin' through, and I got all this energy. Today I flung the covers off and, when I got to my feet, I bent over and tried to touch my toes, like I always do, first thing." He snapped his fingers. "And just like that— I felt like somebody had taken an oil can to my joints. After breakfast, I stood at the kitchen window, sipping my coffee, and staring at the trampoline. I knew I could take on that sucker today; I just felt it in my bones."

Without the puffy suit, Merlin was a gaunt figure, more scarecrow than Michelin Man. Bushy eyebrows and wispy white hair stuck out at all angles. His nose and cheeks were rough and red. I laid my hand on his cold cheek and looked into his eyes, blue as the clear winter sky, hopeful as a child's.

"Maya, how long is this going to last?" Merlin asked.

"I wish I knew, Merlin," I said. "I wish I knew."

CHAPTER 4

NO DIARY FOR YOU

JORN TOLD ME IT was going to happen. Merlin Huus broke his arm two days ago on his granddaughter's trampoline. Jorn's not psychic; he's just irritatingly logical—his mind automatically leaps from old bones to dangerous toy to emergency room. Me, I shoot for the creative and crazy every time. I prefer to think of Merlin bouncing higher and higher, filling with joy like a balloon until he drifts away to a place where old joints never complain and cranky backs are kind.

The Monday class was over. I cast a sad glance toward the spot where Merlin's mat usually was. As the rest of the students stepped out into the darkening night, Jorn hung back. He'd pulled on a University of Missouri sweatshirt and not bothered to smooth down his shaggy hair. Hands stuffed into his pockets, he trailed behind me, up the spiral stairs to the second floor of the fire station, to my home. "Can I see this diary?"

I crossed to the kitchen area and filled a tea kettle with water. "No."

"It's part of the story, according to you."

"There is no story."

"There is always a story," Jorn said and, without an invitation, began exploring my home. He wandered around the living area, leaning close to study the framed photos on the fireplace mantel: images of Sadie and me, laughing, doing yoga on a log; Heart, David, and Sadie crowded into a porch swing; a younger Evie and Larry in hiking boots and backpacks. He turned toward the rest of the room.

"You like color," he said, as if shocked.

I tended to dress in neutrals, a remnant from my year in New York. And I wanted no jarring colors in the yoga studio. It was a place of calm, natural shades; plants, candles, Buddha altar; music sprinkled with chimes, bells, and monks chanting. There you could close your eyes and hear running streams and the wind rushing through the pines along with your own slow, steady breath.

My home was a different matter. It was orange pillows on a red sofa. It was where head-banging tunes and bass-heavy dance jams from the radio replaced subdued Tibetan bells and my well-used DVD collection was evenly split between kung fu movies and *Buffy the Vampire Slayer* (the TV show, *not* the movie).

The walls were exposed brick, the floor hardwood. In the long, open room, rugs separated the kitchen and dining area from the living room—a chili red Oriental rug defined the kitchen, while a handmade curry gold one framed the living room.

"Cushy furniture, large-screen TV, it's all so . . . normal."

"What did you expect?" I said. "A bed of nails?"

As Jorn sat down at the kitchen table and peered into his cup of tea with disgust, he said, "You know, ever since that day at David's house, I've been doing some investigating." He studied my kitchen as if he were memorizing it. "The usual stuff. Internet searches on black cherry trees, shamans, James Tumblethorne, your family."

"Find anything interesting?"

His gaze settled on me. "Your parents are millionaires, and they still grow their own food and repair their own cars."

"Evie hates preservatives. And Larry likes to tinker."

"Evie's the creative mind behind the stories and characters of Skyes the Limit."

"She's an artist."

"Larry's the wizard behind the curtain; he writes the code for the games. Heart's the business brain."

"And who am I?" I asked with a smile.

"You're glaringly missing from Google. Hell, I don't even think you pay taxes."

You had to give Larry credit. When you asked to go off the grid, he *really* wiped you.

"Oh," I said, "I'm sure I'm in there somewhere."

"If you've gone to college . . ."

"Several of them, as a matter of fact."

"Obviously, you didn't get a degree from any of them."

I motioned to the teapot, but Jorn waved away a refill. "And what did you find about Tum?"

He exhaled and leaned back. "Hell's Angel. Liked to booze and brawl. Partial to guns. Quite familiar with the authorities in several states."

"Popular guy."

"Then one day he quits. Rides away from the gang and into your commune. Doesn't leave. Becomes a reformed man. Saw the light, apparently, after joining your merry band. No more fighting. No more weapons charges."

"We can't take all the credit. Tum did some of the work."

"You said he was your nanny?"

"Everyone has a job at Whispering Spirit, something they're good at, and Tum was good with kids."

"Makes sense."

"Why?"

"He practically raised his kid sister."

"I didn't know that." Tum had never spoken of his family. Just his biker days, gory stories to scare us kids and keep us in line, but never the time before that.

"She was a cop, killed during a drug bust, only thirty-three years old. Happened shortly before Tum left the gang."

When Tum joined us, he gave up guns and beer. He even quit smoking, cold turkey. There had been a wildness in him that drew me, but I felt safe with him. Tum came to Whispering Spirit seeking redemption, and, in the end, I think he found it. Still, history cannot be erased. Tum called upon the wounds of his past in doing his shamanic work. He understood weakness and dependency and fear. And that made him a brilliant healer.

I sighed. "I bet Tum was a good brother. He was as loyal and protective as the family dog, but he wouldn't let you get away with stuff. When I was being a brat, complaining about something Heart said to me or how my day had gone all wrong, he would take me up to the meadow to look at the stars. We'd sit there, him as quiet as can be and me talking, talking. Finally, he would turn to me and say, 'Maya, listen to the stars.' And I would look up and forget everything—but just being."

I looked into Jorn's eyes and saw understanding and something else: kindness. He was clearly uncomfortable with my sadness, but he respectfully let my grief lie. Everyone in town knew Jorn had spent the last five years as a war correspondent; his proud uncle had been all too willing to share news of his nephew's exploits. Thus, the bullet wounds. Jorn had seen plenty of death and grief, knew it was not a small thing when life was stolen away, knew it was more than a headline.

"I miss Tum," I said.

We sat in silence.

Jorn unconsciously rubbed his injured shoulder.

"You did too much today," I said, getting up and walking behind him. I stepped into the sphere of his cologne, something subtle and woodsy, and placed a hand on his aching shoulder. He flinched, tensed.

"What are you doing?"

"It's called *reiki*. Energy healing."

Immediately, I felt his injured shoulder begin to respond, hungrily reaching out for energy.

"I don't believe in all this energy stuff," he said, even as he began to relax. After a few minutes, he let out a sigh. "Damn, that feels good."

"There's healing energy all around us," I said conversationally. "I'm just helping your shoulder tap into it."

"Don't ruin this," he muttered.

The shoulder warmed. My hand tingled. Just when I thought he might have fallen asleep, Jorn said, "I found Tumblethorne's obit in a New Mexico paper."

I already knew cause of death. A fire. I didn't want to think of Tum dying in such a horrible way.

"Fell asleep while smoking," Jorn continued. "Sorry."

I straightened. "That's impossible."

"That's the official story."

I whispered. "Tum quit smoking years ago."

Jorn reached for my laptop on the table, booted it up, and began clacking at the keys. "Here it is," he said. Just as I leaned over his shoulder to read the obituary, my cell phone on the counter chimed.

Still keeping a hand on Jorn's shoulder, I grabbed the phone.

"Maya," grumbled a voice I didn't recognize. "This is Nico." It was the lawyer who had ridden all the way from New Mexico on his Harley to deliver Tum's diary. He had clomped up to my door on a February day, leather duster fluttering behind him; beard, eyebrows, and wild hair crusted with ice. His grin was big, and his stories of Tum even bigger. We'd traded tales long into the night, holding our own memorial for Tum, with one beer after another. He'd consumed more pizza than I'd ever seen anyone eat and had looked like a happy giant snoring on my red couch.

Now, he sounded grumpy—and in pain. "Nico, are you all right?"

"I didn't tell them anything, Maya. The bastards. I swear, they got nothin' outta me."

CHAPTER 5

WARNING

W HAT HAPPENED, NICO?" I asked. Jorn turned toward me, eyebrow lifted.

"Bastards jumped me in the alley behind my office. Tried to Taser me, if you can believe that. I knocked some heads."

"Are you hurt?"

"Couple broken ribs, dislocated pinky, mother of a headache. Smacked me in the head with a two-by-four. Been hurt worse getting out of the bathtub."

"Did you recognize them?

"Suits. Fancy suits. Young guys. White butch haircuts." I could imagine Nico shaking his long rust-colored hair out of his eyes. "The Taser-happy bastard had a tattoo on his hand." Silence. "Maya, they wanted Tum's diary."

Shock rippled through me. I circled the table and sat down

with a thud. Jorn leaned toward me and touched my hand, a question in his eyes.

"Why would they want the diary, Nico?"

"Don't know, but Tum was always crazy paranoid about somebody getting it."

"How did they know you had it?"

"That's what's got me worried, Maya. Got a call from Whispering Spirit, too. Someone was there asking questions about Tum. A week ago."

Fear for my friends made my heart thump. "Do you think it was the same guys?"

"I don't know. Only thing I can figure is someone let my name slip. I've been to Whispering Spirit a few times with Tum."

Jorn tapped the computer screen. I nodded. "Nico, had Tum started smoking again?"

I heard a pause and the sound of gulping water. "Perco-set. Gotta love it. Smoking? No, he still believed in all that body-is-a-temple bullshit."

"The newspaper said the fire was caused by Tum smoking in bed."

"It did? Don't remember that, Maya, but it can't be right. Of course, up in the mountains, they don't have your top arson investigators. I thought Tum's death was an accident. Now after that visit from the Butch Twins, I'm not so sure."

My hand gripped the phone. "You think they're responsible for Tum's death?"

"I'll do some snooping." I heard rustling and another groan. "Damn ribs. You watch your back, you hear?"

I hung up. "That was Tum's lawyer," I told Jorn. "Someone is looking for the diary, and they beat up Nico trying to get it."

This unburdening was not like me. I don't involve people in my troubles. I am usually the one sticking my nose into other people's problems. What was it about Jorn? I couldn't figure him out, and I couldn't stop thinking about him. There is something irresistible about a guy who doesn't realize he's wearing one red sock and one black one.

"You could be in danger," he said, rubbing his temple where a bullet had once swiped him.

I doubted that. "They'll never find me or the diary."

"Because you're off the grid."

I nodded.

Jorn tapped the laptop. "Speaking of that, what are you hiding from, Maya?"

CHAPTER 6

WINTER COMES

BEFORE I COULD THINK of a good lie to tell Peter Jorn, someone rapped on my door. I dragged my eyes away from the intent look on Jorn's face. He expected answers, but this was something I didn't talk about with anyone. I jumped up and clattered down the wrought-iron staircase. After a moment, I heard him follow me.

The man on my doorstep was precisely dressed, from his expensive topcoat to his big-heeled boots, which gave him a lift to my height of five seven. He swept off a wool fedora revealing a face of sharp angles and long black hair. It was brushed back from his forehead and came to his shoulders, where it flipped up slightly at the ends. He had a shadow beard, the kind that perturbed me. In my opinion, you either shaved or you didn't. I glanced from the stranger to

Jorn's smooth, clean face and did a double take. Jorn looked furious.

"Yoga studio, right?" the man smiled.

"Yes—"

"Good." He stepped in. I moved back. The man glanced around as he tugged off his leather gloves and unbuttoned his coat, then stopped. "Well, I'll be damned. Peter Jorn."

"Sebastian Winter," Jorn said.

I closed the door and turned to Jorn. Cold vibes poured off him like vapor from dry ice in a bowl of water, sliding over the edge and creeping across the floor toward me and this confident stranger. My gaze shifted from one man to the other.

"Heard you took a few in Afghanistan." The man looked Jorn over.

Jorn held himself straighter. "Nothing I couldn't handle."

"And now you run a small-town newspaper."

"And you own a media empire."

Winter dipped his head in a gesture of false modesty. "We've both come so far."

When Jorn took a step toward him, Sebastian Winter threw up his hands with a laugh. "Come, Peter, let's not fight."

I said, "How do you two know each other?"

"College," Jorn said.

"Roomies actually. Our freshman year." Winter began strolling around the room, examining the cubicles, the mats, Evie's painting of a lotus on the wall. He stopped. "Is that flower eating someone?"

It was entirely possible. Evie's art could best be described as magnificent and troubling. She specialized in serene moments with an edge: a spider crawling out of a bowl of chicken noodle soup, a boat on a placid sea reflected in the eye of a killer whale, a smiling owl with a handlebar moustache and big teeth. She always painted animals or flowers, and they always seemed to know something you didn't, something dark and mysterious, and, perhaps, not of this world.

Winter cleared his throat and looked away from the painting. "Yes, umm, University of Missouri." He nodded toward Jorn's ratty sweatshirt. "We worked on the J-School newspaper together. When Peter wasn't editing the campus rag. What was it called again? *The Tiger?* No, *The Maneater.*"

As it happened, I had spent a few semesters at Missouri, studying art history that time. I knew the journalism school was a big jewel in the university's crown and one of the only journalism schools in the country to publish a daily city newspaper that actually competed with the local city newspaper. It was called the *Columbia Missourian.* The *Missourian* liked sticking it to the city paper, and the *Maneater*, a free tabloid written for and by students, liked sticking it to the *Missourian. Maneater* reporters who were journalism majors were required to work on the *Missourian* as well.

"What are you doing here, Sebastian?" Jorn said in a low voice.

"I'll be in town for a while," Sebastian stopped before me, paused, "and I didn't want to miss my yoga."

"You didn't come to Gabriel's Garden for yoga." Jorn stepped closer to me. At six one, he towered over Sebastian. Sebastian's grin didn't waver.

Keeping his eyes on Sebastian, Jorn made the introductions, "Maya Skye, this is Sebastian Winter, of Winter Media."

Winter Media. I'd heard of it. Who hadn't? Winter Media owned supermarket tabloids, online tell-all sites, and news programs staffed with quasi-journalists, talking heads, and conservative commentators whose remarks inflamed Larry and Evie and made dinner conversations about politics a treat. Truth benders, Evie called them. Vicious opinion hiding behind the banner of news, Larry said. Winter Media was in the forefront of a disturbing era in journalism—reporting with an agenda.

Winter ignored Jorn. Continuing to assess me, he drummed his fingers on the brim of the hat in his hand. "Do you give private classes?"

The fog of Jorn's cold vibes crept up to my knees. I sneaked a quick glance at him. "Sure," I said, handing Sebastian a schedule of classes. He gave a nod, rebuttoned his camel hair coat, and, with a satisfied smile, turned away.

As he reached the door, he paused with gloved hand on the knob and looked over his shoulder at Jorn. "I'm staying at the Strawberry B&B if you want to catch up, Peter."

"It's different this time, Sebastian."

"I don't think so."

"This is my town. My story."

Sebastian laughed. "We'll see." He placed the fedora on his head, and with a tug on the brim, he tipped his hat to me and stepped out into the March bluster.

With Sebastian's exit, frosty air swept across the room, making me shiver. I sat down on the stairs and pulled my sweater closer. I patted the step beside me. "You want to tell me about him?"

Jorn hesitated then lowered himself carefully onto the

step. His shoulder touched mine. Elbows on knees, he clasped his hands in front of him. He didn't look at me. "Stay away from him, Maya."

"Why?"

"He's got a Napoleon complex."

"I noticed the elevator shoes."

"It's not just that. He can't be trusted."

I waited.

Jorn ran his hands through his shaggy blond hair and looked at his feet. For the first time, he noticed his socks didn't match. "What the—," he blew out a resigned gust of air. After several moments, he began, "I was working on a story for the *Missourian*. A fake concert scam. Sebastian stole my notes and ran the story under his byline."

"What did you do?"

"I got even. The next time I had a scoop, I left my notes lying around again, but they didn't tell the whole story."

"You fed Sebastian disinformation."

"I ran the real story in the *Maneater*."

"And Sebastian ran the fake story," I said.

"The *Missourian* editor wasn't happy with Sebastian or being scooped by the *Maneater*."

"So you were rivals."

"Columbia is a small college town swarming with eager young reporters. Every one of them wants to break the next Watergate. Everyone's a rival. The *Missourian* and the *Maneater* have always fought for the same stories."

The bizarre blooming of the cherry tree had attracted numerous calls from the press. Heart had hung up on more than one reporter. Could Sebastian really be in town for a story about a mixed-up tree? Seemed below his pay scale.

"What do you think Sebastian's really after?"

Jorn turned his head, and for a moment, I got lost in his worried blue eyes. "I don't know, but we better find out."

CHAPTER 7

WHY I HATE ICE FISHING

S CARY? I'LL TELL YOU something. There are a lot of things
scarier than you. And I'm one of them."

That was my best Buffy the Vampire Slayer imitation.
I'm standing in front of the mirror in the bathroom, my
body at an angle, with no mercy in my eye. My fists are up
by my face. I'm wearing the usual: loose yoga pants and a
skinny tank top. My long brunette hair, with the auburn
highlights Heart just put in, is pulled back into a ponytail.
As usual, strands escape and fall around my face. It makes
me look tough. Then I lean forward, stretch my mouth into
a fake smile, and reach for my toothbrush.

I have been playing superhero for as long as I can remember.

I'm not into heroes, like Batman, who need gadgets to survive. I'm more like the Grasshopper in *Kung Fu,* that old television show—peaceful yet deadly. But let's not talk about that.

I woke up in a kick-ass mood, and it continued throughout the day and into the late afternoon when I took a walk around the city lake. It was snowing, and I loved walking in the snow, even if it was only ten degrees. So around five, when the day was about to snap shut and night hovered at the gate, I circled the city lake on a snow-packed trail. The wind wasn't bad in the shelter of the trees; still, I was layered like an onion. Snowflakes filled the air, meandering their way to earth. I was humming the Stones' "Sympathy for the Devil" when I came around a curve and saw them.

Out on the lake, three teenage boys squatted around a hole in the ice. Their laughter drifted across the lake toward me. At first, I thought they were ice fishing. But if they were fishing, it was pretty low-tech. Basically, they had dropped a rope in a hole. No pole, no canvas stools or the poor fisherman's equivalent—a plastic bucket. I watched one boy haul the rope out. At the end of it was a bag. He poked it, which his buddies thought was funny. That's when I saw something in the bag move.

Without thinking, I leaped off the path.

I slid down the small snowy bank on my rear and started across the ice, slipping every which way, until my legs recalled the stealth of ice walking.

"Hey!" I shouted.

The boys glanced my way and slowly rose. They were all taller than I. In their parkas and puffy gloves, each one looked as if he could play for the Vikings. One wore a woolen ski mask with holes for the eyes and mouth, the kind popular with people up to no good. He's the one who said, "Whaddya want?"

"I want to see what's in the bag," I said, stopping a few feet from them.

"Fuck off," said the boy holding the dripping sack. Already rime was forming over it in the cold air. It was one of those reusable grocery tote bags tree huggers kept handy for the occasional shopping spree. I owned several. The top of the sack was tied shut by a bright yellow nylon rope. A pitiful sound issued from the sack.

"Not going to happen, guys," I said. I stood my ground and tried to look brave. Always appear calm and like the one willing to bust some heads, Tum used to say in our training sessions. Once, years ago, I was calm all the way through, from the cool steel in my gray eyes to the steady beat in my heart. Once I walked into danger without fear. But things have happened since then. On this day, alone, on a frozen lake with three unfriendly strangers, I was not as fearless as I appeared.

The boy with the mask studied me. I stared back. Eyes always looked cruel through the slits of a mask. Slowly, he smiled at me and stuck out his tongue, which was pierced. Having several piercings in my ears and one in my belly button, I wasn't impressed. We were maybe five feet away from each other. I took a step toward the boys and held out my gloved hand. "Give me the bag." Another lesson from Tum: Don't let them build up their courage. Surprise and strike. No chit-chat.

At this time of day, the lake was deserted. Most people were at home, peering into the refrigerator, thinking about dinner. The light was quickly fading, the temperature dropping. The boys exchanged glances, and my muscles tensed. I slowly slid into a fighting stance, creating a narrower target, softening my knees, keeping my arms loose and ready at my side. My pulse thudded in my head.

"Sure," said the boy with the bag. He was shorter than the other two and better dressed. He wore jeans and a ski jacket, a lift ticket still dangling from the zipper tab. Long dishwater blond curls stuck out from under his bright orange knit cap. Snowboard Boy. He pretended to hand the bag over, then, at the last moment, dropped it back into the hole.

"Go fish, bitch," he said. With that, the three took off running, their laughter echoing in the growing night.

"No!" I screamed and dived for the rope rapidly disappearing into the hole. I tugged off my gloves as I belly-flopped on the ice and grabbed for the rope. It raced through my hands, the fibers burning my fingers. I tried to tighten my grip, but my hands were already freezing, and my muscles refused to respond. Both arms were up to the elbow in the icy black water when, finally, the rope stopped sliding.

When danger is close enough to tap me on the shoulder, time slows down for me. So what followed probably took only seconds, but it felt longer.

I couldn't seem to make my fingers work to pull the rope up, hand over hand. My arms were as heavy as bricks. So I began scooting back along the ice, tugging the rope with me. Wiggle, pull. Wiggle, pull. I was panting. My breath caught when my arms came out of the water and hit the cold air. Sweat trickled under my wool cap. But I didn't let go, and eventually, I saw the top of the green bag. When it reached the edge of the hole, I gave a jerk and it flipped out onto the ice.

On my knees, I fumbled with the knot cinching the bag closed. "C'mon," I whispered. The wet bag was heavier than I expected, and I realized there were rocks at the bottom. There was no movement in the bag.

Finally, I got the bag open, reached in, and pulled out a sopping wet kitten. Sympathy shot through my heart. Its fur was matted against its tiny head, and its eyes were closed. I immediately began massaging it with shivering fingers. My teeth had begun to chatter. No sign of life. What do I do? For a moment, I panicked and just knelt there, crying.

Then I began rubbing the soaked creature with my dry gloves. "C'mon, baby, c'mon."

I looked around me for help and was shocked to see Sebastian Winter standing across the lake, at the edge, in his expensive coat and hat. His gloved hands were clasped in front of him, and he was just staring at me. I raised my hand, but he didn't respond.

I turned to the kitten again and desperately searched for signs of life. Finally, I whipped off my Sherpa hat, gently tucked the kitten inside it, and lifted the hat to my face. I blew warm breath into the hat, over and over. I had some idea that if I could just create a chamber of warmth . . . And then I heard the tiniest sound ever. A mew so soft. I brought the hat up to my ear and felt a faint puff of air from the kitten's wet snout. I quickly wrapped the earflaps of the hat around the kitten, swaddling it tightly, then unzipped my coat and fleece, and stuffed the bundle down the front of my shirt, between my thermal underwear and my chest.

As I got up, smiling with relief and triumph, I looked toward Sebastian, but he was gone. I searched the banks of the lake. They were empty. It had grown darker and colder. I realized I couldn't feel my fingers anymore. If I didn't get the kitten and me inside soon, we'd both be dead. With one hand clutching the kitten securely to my chest, I scooped up my gloves and ran across the frozen lake, not toward my house but toward Heart's. Big sister's house was closer, and she had a heating pad.

WE SPENT THE NIGHT—HEART, Sadie, and I—in Heart's cozy kitchen, watching a half-dead kitten sleep. We wrapped it in a heating pad and tucked it in a shoebox. None of us had a clue if it would make it. At one point, I suggested putting the kitten in the oven.

"Maya!" Sadie was aghast. "You can't cook her!"

"To warm her," I said. "Put the oven on low. Like two hundred."

Heart gave me a stern look. "No cats in my oven."

I was exhausted. Wearing some of Heart's dry thermal underwear and two sweaters, I rested my head in my arms on the table. The kitten slept. It was such a small, helpless thing. Being on that lake, facing the boys, had prodded old memories. I'd come to the rescue of a small, helpless thing before. A woman. A cry for help snagging me off a busy New York sidewalk. That time I'd rushed down an alley.

No thought to danger; no thought to consequences. I ran into a darkness of my own making, a darkness that follows me to this day.

When I slammed into the side of the man, his fist raised to hit the woman again, I just wanted to stop him. I didn't really have a plan beyond distraction. Maybe scare him off; witnesses were never good. But he came back at both of us. He landed a punch to my jaw; my head snapped back, but I didn't lower my own fists. I warded off one punch, another, trying to find my opening. Then there it was: he made a slight turn toward the whimpering woman curled in a pile of trash and trying to withdraw further from this nightmare. I put everything I had into the side kick. The man flew against the brick wall and stuck there, as if glued. His eyes looked at me in surprise. I took a step forward. His body went lax, and his head dropped to his chest.

I frowned, puzzled, then I saw it. The piece of rusted rebar. It was protruding from the old brick wall, about chest height, a perfect tool to hang a hat on or impale a man.

That's how quickly the world can change. One moment you are strolling amid the night lights of a big city, happy, free, not really thinking at all, and the next you have taken a life. And you can't stop thinking.

You have killed.

You have dimmed the world. When all you have ever wanted to do was add to this sublime existence. You have ripped a massive hole in your karmic fabric. You have violated the yogic principle of *ahimsa*—do no harm to any creature. To someone raised as I was, it was a devastating realization.

I helped the battered and bloody woman to stand, waving away her thanks again and again. As we parted ways, we were both crying, for different reasons.

I staggered home and called Evie and Larry in near hysterics. I killed a man, I sobbed. It was an accident, crooned Evie. I'll take care of it, said Larry. To my protective, ever security-conscious father, taking care of it meant keeping me out of the hands of the law. So Larry made me disappear; I no longer existed. With a fake passport, I ran from the events in that New York alley to India to the ashram of Guru Bob. There, I was sure I would find what I had lost. But I didn't. That was seven years ago. I am thirty-five now, and my actions on that night still follow me. I still smell the rubbish; I still see the man's eyes; I still feel the rough brick against my forehead as I leaned against the wall and wept.

I LIFTED MY HEAD from the cradle of my arms on the kitchen table and looked into a pair of slightly crossed blue eyes. Now that the kitten's fur had dried, I realized it had some Siamese in it. It was a champagne shade with brown-tipped tail and ears.

I nudged my eight-year-old niece awake and nodded toward our patient. "What will you name her?"

"Really?" Sadie threw her arms around my neck. Heart, standing in the morning light at the counter, paused as she poured steaming water from a teapot into two cups. She raised an eyebrow.

"Thanks, Maya," she said.

Heart is not a pet person. I blame it on that month when

she was assigned to feed the chickens at Whispering Spirit. She let those hens run all over her.

I shrugged. "What's a sister for?"

CHAPTER 8

THERE WERE NEVER SUCH UNDEVOTED SISTERS

HOW WAS I TO know that David was allergic to cats? Sadie cried when I had to take the feline Popsicle, which she had named Bellarina, to my house. But what could we do? David started sneezing the moment he walked into the kitchen, high-decibel expulsions that made us all jump. For such a small thing, Bella packed a punch.

She also turned out to be a resilient little creature. She was barely in my house twenty-four hours before she was running things. At first, she was baffled by the spiral stairs and mewed until I carried her up them, but soon she was racing up and down the stairs and dangling upside down from them. If the stairs were Bella's personal jungle gym, the hardwood floors were her ice rink. She got going so fast that when she tried to stop, she tumbled rear over head and slid under the rug. She was a speedy ball of fur everywhere but the yoga studio. There she was a different cat. Mysterious. Secretive. She moved calmly around the edges of the large space, dusting the walls with her tail. Her favorite spot was under the table behind my mat, where she could watch the class with a Sphinx-like solemnity.

In addition to Bella, the Monday afternoon yoga class had gained two new people: Sebastian Winter and Sasha Danilova, the visiting sister of Julia Lune. The first time Sasha met Bella she picked up the kitten, which was rubbing its ears on Sasha's handbag; held the cat in front of her face; and said in a stern voice, "No using the expensive Prada for a scratching post, sugar." Bella got one snoot full of Sasha's strong perfume and sneezed until Sasha dropped her to the floor.

While Bella steered clear of Sasha after that, she liked Sebastian Winter, for some reason, and he liked her. He never flinched when she climbed up his silk pants with her sharp little claws. As soon as he entered the studio, he scooped her up, laid her like a blanket over his arm, and began stroking her. "I love cats," he told me. "I always wanted one, but Mother claimed she was allergic. Of course, she wasn't, but I didn't know that when I was little."

"What about a dog?" I asked.

"Mother didn't like those either. And dogs just aren't the same. They're followers. Where's the challenge in that?"

I'd grown up with numerous dogs and cats. Whispering Spirit never turned away a stray.

Sebastian said, "I'm glad you saved this little one."

"So you did see me that day on the lake," I said.

"Yes."

"Yet, you didn't help me."

"You had everything under control." Sebastian smiled down at the purring kitten in his arms. "I went after the boys but lost them."

I didn't know whether to believe him or not.

IT WAS A THURSDAY, and Bella had been a maniac since she woke me at 5:00 A.M. ready to play. Finally, I wore her out with an incessant game of chase the feather on the end of the stick. Curled in a ball in the middle of the bed, Bella was down for the count. I was just about to crawl in beside her for an afternoon nap when the phone rang. It was a desperate-sounding Julia Lune. "I need help," she said.

I found Julia in her office, a small backyard studio connected to her house by a series of tiered decks. It was an adult-size dollhouse with large round windows peering out onto Julia's private lake, which had that frozen look of isolation that water assumes in Minnesota winters. This was where Julia the romance writer dreamed up her sassy dialogue and steamy scenes. There was nothing cold about Julia's writing.

Or her decorating. The office, which had walls of tightly packed bookcases in every direction, was awash in passionate shades from the merlot wool rug to Julia's deep purple alpaca shawl draped across a big leather sofa. Photos overlapped each other on a large magnetic board over the desk. Not one of them was of her husband, Jean-Luc. Mostly, they featured jaw-droppingly sexy men: muscle-bound firemen with no shirts, scrumptiously sculpted doctors with no shirts, hot-bodied archeologists with no shirts.

The room also was plastered with Post-It Notes—on the books, the windowsills, the laptop computer, the chiseled face of a hunk. Don't ever mess with Julia's notes. Ranging from plot ideas to reminders to pick up Jean-Luc's dry cleaning, they kept Julia on track. Once she told me that all her heroines were her alter egos; they looked nothing like her, never left their cell phone in the refrigerator, and were fully capable of turning down a Kit Kat bar. "My readers have dreamy standards," she said. "They want their women cute and spunky, and their men steamy and mysterious."

Today Julia was making no pretense of emulating her heroines. The tendrils escaping her chignon appeared more forlorn than stylish, and she clutched a candy bar in each hand. I leaned across the leather sofa and gently pried one of the chocolate bars from her fingers. I placed the melting blob on the coffee table in front of us and out of reach.

"Okay, what's wrong?" I asked.

"I want you to get rid of her," said Julia, her eyes intent on mine, peering desperately through chocolate-smudged round glasses in black frames. She took another bite.

"Her?"

"Sasha."

At thirty-two, Sasha was ten years younger than her sister Julia and the baby of the seven Danilov children. A petite package of Southern sass, Sasha dressed like a Powder Puff girl with an addiction to Prada and pink. She had already been through three rich husbands.

"Why?" I inched closer to Julia. "What has she done?"

"She's been just . . ." Julia swept a lock of hair from her eye, letting out an exasperated sigh and leaving a streak of chocolate on her cheek. "I never thought my prayer would feel like this. I had forgotten how *Sasha* she is."

"Back up," I said. "This all began with the cleansing ceremony we did last month?"

Julia nodded, loosening more strands of hair. "I was feeling low, that desperate-for-sun feeling. Every year February hits me like this—and I just wanted it to go away. I was missing warm North Carolina and lonesome for family, for someone who drops their G's, for crying out loud."

"And then Sasha appears on your doorstep."

"Out of the blue. I hadn't seen her in months. She'd missed the family gathering at Thanksgiving, which was like breaking twenty-nine laws in my mother's eyes. If I can drag Jean-Luc down to Carolina for my mother's borscht, which he hates, Sasha can haul her size-two butt out of the spa du jour and get on a plane."

"Julia, I don't know if the ceremony really had anything to do with this . . ."

Julia held up a hand. "All I know is I wrote, 'Family, please,' on that paper we burned and Sasha shows up, standing in my foyer in a snow bunny pink parka, Uggs, and enough luggage for an ocean crossing."

Julia reached for the Kit Kat I'd dislodged from her grasp earlier. She froze as the door to the office flew open, and Sasha sauntered in on a wave of cold air. Julia's sister didn't bother to remove her boots at the door as I had, as was the tradition in every household in Minnesota in the wintertime. Crossing the room to the sitting area where we were, Sasha left a trail of snow prints on the Oriental rug. She unzipped her pink parka, plopped down into the wingback chair across from us, and swung a leg over the arm of the chair.

She lifted an eyebrow at the candy wrappers on the coffee table. "Julia, you'll never get into that size-sixteen dress I just bought you if you keep sneakin' those bad boys. Flowing fabrics can only cover so much, sugar."

I started to say, "It's mine," but Julia laid a hand on my arm.

"I do not sneak," she said, straightening, but not releasing the Kit Kat bar.

Sasha tilted her head, her blonde hair rippling around her face. "Sugar, you came out of the womb sneakin' chocolate." Spanish moss dripped from every word.

Wiggling in the chair, settling in for some girl talk, Sasha turned toward me and smiled. "You've got some nice scenery in that yoga class of yours. Tell me about this Jorn fella." She fanned her hand in front of her face as if trying to cool herself. "Whew. I'd like to show him a pose or two."

I ignored the funny feeling in my chest. When I noticed Sasha watching me, I made myself slow my breath. In class, Sasha positions her mat right behind Jorn. She pays more attention to his Down Dog than her own.

"Or maybe Sebastian Winter's more your type." Sasha's grin was wicked. "Mr. Cool. Money. Smart dresser. Maya, sugar, he'll eat you alive."

"Don't bet on that, Sasha." I stared her down.

Sasha laughed. "Are all yoga teachers so hands-on?"

Julia cut in. "Sasha, stop."

Suddenly, Sasha grew bored with the game. She glanced around the room then out the window at the bleak landscape. "Minnesota nice?" she pouted. "Minnesota boring. When is this godforsaken snow gonna leave?"

"May," Julia and I said at the same time.

Sasha's eyes widened. "May!"

I shrugged.

"I'm gonna need more clothes," Sasha said.

As the door closed behind Sasha, silence filled up the space and eased away the tension until there was nothing left of Sasha but a trace of her Joy perfume.

"Look out, Mall of America," I said.

Julia bit off a hunk of candy bar and chewed. I had never seen someone look so miserable while eating chocolate. "My family never comes here, you know. This is the end of the world to them."

"I had no idea."

"That's why I was so happy when I first saw Sasha. I thought, we'll shop in The Cities and go to plays and eat out . . ."

"Sister stuff." I understood. "All those things sound perfect for Sasha."

"But she seems distracted this visit. Something's on her mind. Maybe she's having trouble hooking husband number four."

"And when Sasha is distracted, she is cruel."

"Sasha has never been sugar sweet. She likes her world a

certain way, and women of my size don't fit well into that world."

Poor Julia. She didn't know how romance-novel cute she was in her smudged glasses, frazzled appearance, and normally spunky attitude. With every word she wrote, Julia *was* her heroines.

She gave me a half-hearted smile. "I know I'm being silly. Sasha may like to surround herself with beautiful things, but she also is very generous."

I doubted that, and it must have shown on my face.

"She likes spending money and giving gifts. Expensive gifts. She's a big tipper. She's been that way ever since she was a child."

I asked, "Were you and Sasha close as kids?"

"I thought we were. She had trouble sleeping at night so I made up bedtime stories for her: princesses and knights. She *loved* my stories. Now—" Julia shrugged. Her shoulders slumped, and her eyes looked weary. "Maya, I got to admit, facing that size two every morning is getting me down."

I hugged her. "Do you want me to kick her butt for you?"

Julia pulled back and laughed. "You? The Karma Queen? Whatever happened to helping us all find our inner peace? Besides, Sasha fights dirty."

I didn't tell Julia: so do I.

On the way home, I considered the coincidental events of the past weeks: a blooming cherry tree, a septuagenarian turned gymnast, and now a Southern Cruella De Vil dropped right into our laps.

In my world, coincidence always has an agenda. As Tum used to say, "Coincidence is Spirit trying to get your attention."

Entering the house, distracted by my thoughts, unwrapping my two yards of scarf, I stopped.

Someone had wrecked my place.

CHAPTER 9

I WANT
MY STUFF BACK

B ELLA!" I SHOUTED. RUSHING through the studio, I left a trail on the floor: scarf, gloves, hat, coat. Over and over, I called her name as I searched the cubbyholes where students stored their gear and Bella sometimes curled up for a nap. I squatted and rummaged through the piles of yoga mats and blocks scattered all over the foyer. I took the stairs by twos and skidded to a halt at the top.

No way four pounds of fur could have done this: furniture was overturned, books ripped from the shelves. Drawers from the desk and the kitchen had been upended onto the floor. Cabinet doors stood open. Up to my ankles in frozen food and pillow stuffing, I yelled, "Bellarina!"

I heard a sound. It came from the bedroom. I tiptoed to the door, which was slightly ajar. I nudged it open, then fell back into defensive mode with my fists up near my face. Nobody came rushing at me. I cautiously stepped inside and began wading through the clothes scattered everywhere.

"Meowwwww." I spun to the closet and opened it with care.

"Meowwwww." Bella sounded mad, and with good reason. Someone had trapped her in one of my green recyclable grocery bags, tied it closed with a shoelace, and flung her in the closet. I grabbed the bag, sank into a nest of clothes on the floor, and began working on the knot in the lace with trembling fingers.

"Why are people always putting you in bags?" I grumbled. When I finally liberated Bella, I held her close and tried to calm her. I kissed the top of her head. But she was having none of it. She leaped from my arms and began pacing all around me. Her tail lashed angrily. She was a loud complainer.

"I'm sorry I wasn't here to protect you," I said.

Now that I knew Bella was safe, reality struck. I felt weak. I leaned my arms on my knees and rubbed my face. I took a few moments to pull myself together then got up to assess the damage. The refrigerator door was open. A six-pack of beer was gone. Another glance toward the living room, and I saw my computer was no longer on the sofa. My flat screen had been ripped from the wall.

That's when it hit me: the diary.

I flew to the stairs, nearly tripping over a still-pacing, still-furious Bella. I stumbled down the steps and ran to the yoga room. Bella followed, complaining all the way. There wasn't much to search or wreck in the empty studio, but still I needed to check on the diary. I pulled the table away from the wall, fumbled with the loose bricks until I dislodged them, and reached inside the hole. My fingers touched silk, and I sighed with relief. I pulled the diary from its hiding place, leaned back against the brick wall, and clasped it to my chest.

The diary was safe.

I slipped off the rubber band and opened it. The smell of the sea wafted into the room.

"What the hell?"

"WTF, Maya?"

Jorn and Olivia stood in the doorway.

GABRIEL'S GARDEN DOESN'T NEED a large police force, and fingerprint specialists certainly don't fit into the town's budget. The officer who answered the call doubted finger-printing would have helped anyway. There were so many fingerprints downstairs from my students it probably looked like the walls of a kindergarten craft room. As Officer Holmes scribbled in his little report book, he held out little hope of getting my electronics back. "Probably already in a Twin Cities pawn shop by now," he said. As for the beer, he doubted it made it outside the city limits.

"Probably kids," the officer said, eyeing Olivia as she restacked the yoga mats and blocks. Olivia sometimes just dropped by after school. I didn't ask too many questions about her life, and I let her do her homework in a quiet cor-ner of the yoga studio when I didn't have a class.

I'd called Heart and my parents. They were upstairs with Jorn, righting furniture and putting the silverware back in its drawer. My father had arrived with a new laptop. He was already gleefully reinstalling programs and accounts, pulling information from a cloud somewhere.

Finally, Officer Holmes left, and I sent Olivia home with a hug. I joined my family and Jorn upstairs. Evie, sitting at the table, was soothing Bella on her lap, while Heart bustled in the kitchen, making soup. Emotionally spent, I sank into one of the kitchen chairs, the diary still clutched to my chest.

"You must feel so violated," Heart said, stirring a large pot on the stove then turning back to the chopping board. "Vegetable soup is just what you need. It's your favorite, right?"

No, potato leek soup was my comfort food, but nothing was stopping Heart from creating some form of culinary comfort. Cooking calmed Heart and set her world aright. Once when we were young, I talked Heart into taking a drag from a reefer I'd liberated from one of the commune papas. I'd found her later, guilt-stricken and high, in the community kitchen, up to her twelve-year-old elbows in avocados and tomatoes. We had chips and guac for days.

While Heart found her center in the kitchen, I found mine in chanting. I wanted nothing more than to be alone and whisper words of peace and love and gratitude, to let the repetition sink into me until it calmed my quivering insides. But I couldn't just kick out my family. Jorn, but not my family.

I caught Jorn studying me, and I crossed my eyes at him. "Careful," he said, "or they'll stay that way."

"Don't you have a home?"

71

"Yours is more exciting."

Bella rose from Evie's lap, arched her back in a perfect Cat Pose, then leaped to the floor and walked over to the couch. She soundlessly jumped to the back of the sofa and hunkered down behind Larry's shoulder, her tail sweeping around his neck like a scarf.

"I'm going to install a security system in this place," he said, not looking up from the keyboard. "There's stuff out there that will blow your mind."

"Larry, we just want her to be safe, not living in a fortress," Evie said.

"But this stuff is so cool," Larry said. "I'm installing a tracker on this laptop so if someone takes this one, we've got him."

"Keep it simple." Evie gave him an indulgent but no-nonsense look.

"I can do simple." When Evie continued to give him The Look, he threw up his hands, frightening Bella into a back-flip off the sofa. "Simple, I got it."

"Come and get it," Heart sang. She began ladling soup into bowls and handing them to Jorn. He looked lost for a moment and then started placing them around the table. Evie brought out spoons and napkins. Heart pulled out a tray of warm French bread from the oven. The last time I had seen that loaf it was lying on the kitchen floor, thawing, in a puddle of other half-frozen food.

I hate to admit it, but Heart had been right. Something warm and simple was just what I had needed. The thought of someone pawing through my things gave me the creeps, and I still wasn't able to let the diary out of my sight. Jorn kept eyeing it but so far hadn't mentioned it. I was mad and afraid, two emotions that do not mix well in me.

About halfway through the meal, my phone rang. I pulled it from my pocket. It was Nico.

"Just got an interesting offer," he said. "As your attorney, I have to advise you of it."

"You're my attorney now?"

"Somebody's got to have your back, kid," Nico growled.

"What's the offer?"

"One mill for the diary."

"Whoa. Who?"

"An anonymous offer."

"Does this stink as much as I think it does?" I asked.

"To high heaven."

I glanced at Jorn, who was leaning toward me. "Was it one of the guys who attacked you?" I asked.

"Nope. A woman."

I told Nico about my house being tossed and my cat being stashed in a grocery bag.

"Sorry about the cat," Nico said.

"This sort of pisses me off," I said.

"Understandable. So that's a no on the mill?"

"That's a no," I said.

"Be in touch." Nico rang off.

Everyone at the table was looking at me. "Someone wants to buy the diary for a million bucks," I said.

Larry's eyebrows lifted. Evie sat back, her calm eyes on me. Heart smiled. "Sell! What are you waiting for? Get that cursed thing out of your house and out of our lives. In fact, just give it to him."

"You know I can't do that."

"Because Tum left it to you," Heart said.

"Because I'm the keeper now."

Heart put her spoon down with a clatter. "That damn diary is going to bring trouble down on all of us. I've got a family to think of, Maya."

"I won't let anything happen to you, David, or Sadie."

"Like that is supposed to make me feel better. You can't even keep your cat safe."

Evie stepped in. "Now, Heart."

"Don't 'Now, Heart' me, Evie. Real people are breaking into real homes."

"We can't choose other people's paths for them," Evie said.

Heart stood. "This is not just about her. People are coming after that book. And I don't want my family in the crossfire." She turned from Evie to me. "They've already been inside your house. If that doesn't freaking scare you . . ." She shook her head.

Yes, it scared me, more than I would let any of them see. I watched Heart leave, listened as she grabbed her coat off the hooks by the front door and pulled on her boots. She slammed the door behind her. Then, abruptly, it opened again, and Heart's shout came up the stairs, "Lock this damn door behind me. This isn't Whispering Freaking Spirit."

Evie and Larry soon followed, going off into the night, arms around each other, heads bent in discussion. I watched them from the door for a moment then went back upstairs. I dropped onto the sofa. Jorn joined me.

"You're not going to write about this, are you?"

"Two lines in the police report. Nobody reads the police report," he assured me.

"Everybody reads the police report."

We both stared at the diary lying in my lap.

"What's in there that's so important?" he asked.

I shrugged. I opened the book and caught a whiff of bubblegum.

"A treasure map?" Jorn asked.

I shook my head.

"The truth about who killed Kennedy?"

I flipped the page and the scent of smoke twisted around us.

"Do you smell that?"

"What?"

"Smoke."

Jorn looked toward the kitchen. "I don't smell anything."

I let my head drop back against the sofa. Bella leaped into my lap and curled up on the opened diary.

Jorn cleared his throat. "I could stay the night." I turned to look at him. He lifted his hands. "On the couch."

"I'm not afraid," I said, although I was.

He nodded.

Bella and I walked him to the door. He piled on his layers then waited outside the door until he heard the dead bolt. As I climbed the stairs, I was already chanting.

That night I slept with the diary and Bella. We all needed comfort. I fell asleep reading the diary, its words and scents winding through my dreams.

The next morning, I chanted, meditated, and finished reading the diary. Then I replaced it in its hiding place.

I had to keep it safe. Because now I knew its secrets.

CHAPTER 10

THE WHISPERINGS OF SECRETS

IT WAS LATE MARCH, and we were entering the cherry tree's fourth week in full bloom. Merlin's arm was still mending, and his daughter had dismantled the trampoline. Both Merlin and his granddaughter were gloomy about that. Sitting in lotus on my bed, I studied the diary. Bella was stretched out beside me, looking twice as long as she actually was. When the phone rang, I had to dig it out from under her.

It was Heart. "Have you sold the diary yet?"

"No."

She hung up without saying good-bye. We'd had this conversation several times since the burglary a week ago. I regretted the cleansing ceremony, involving my students. The diary was full of many things I didn't understand or didn't want to understand. It held seasonal complaints, sad entries, and frightening chronicles—of crops failing, of babies who never came, of a woman tossed from a roof when she refused to hand over the diary. Men and women had given up those they loved rather than put them in harm's way—because of the diary. I had no idea if these things were true. Maybe they were the shamanic equivalent of old wives' tales.

Or maybe Heart was right. Maybe I had no business bringing this into my house, my family, my town.

There were stories of the diary's keepers being hunted and chased, of monasteries in snowy mountains, of fire and ice. I found a page with a bullet hole in it. A single page. How could that happen? I sniffed the page, expecting gunpowder, and smelled nail polish instead.

Some entries were as mundane as: "Had mangos for breakfast. Yum." One keeper wrote bad doggerel, while another argued existential theories. Propped up in my bed with the diary on my lap, I waded through everything from grocery lists to naughty limericks about the good folks from Nantucket. And with each turn of the page, new smells drifted up, surrounded me, and clung to my fingers: the soft scent of talcum powder, the musty smell of marijuana, the aroma of new leather.

Then I came across several references that had me sitting up with interest. Different keepers in different decades in different lands. The same reference, the same phrase. In different languages. *Vida eterna. Immortalité.* Eternal life.

I thumbed back and forth, rereading one section and then another, making sure I was interpreting the words correctly. As the night wore on, my spirits sank lower. There was no way to tell if what the diary said was true. But did that really matter? If someone believed it was true, believed that this book held some great secret to eternal life, that person might be willing to resort to—anything.

It could all be nonsense, a wild goose chase that had driven men and women to extremes over the decades.

But if it was real . . . I was in deep shit.

The phone rang again. Heart, no doubt, trying to wear me down as she used to do when we were kids. When she wanted something, there was no stopping her.

But this time it was Nico.

"She raised her offer," he said.

"You're kidding."

"Five million."

I nearly dropped the phone. "Wow."

Now, I have never been a person who needed much. That whole scoffing-at-materialism thing was the air we breathed at Whispering Spirit. In our family, money was to be used to help others. And with five million, I could do a lot of good. I could vaccinate children in Africa and buy llamas for farmers in Peru.

"Maya, you still there?"

"Yeah."

"What do you think?"

"That's a lot of llamas."

"Huh?"

I mentioned the name of a nonprofit organization that gave livestock to Third World farmers to help them climb out of poverty.

"Feed the world," Nico said, "I see where you're heading."

He began rambling about social investing and the stock market and how he could handle all the paperwork.

I broke into his litany of plans for my windfall. "Do you think she offered Tum money?"

There was a pause on the line.

"It wouldn't have done any good," he said.

"Because he was the keeper."

"Yeah."

I felt the diary calling to me, whispers of responsibility twisting and looping around me.

"Does she think you have the diary? Does she know about me?" I was already making a mental to-do list for Larry. He loved putting up firewalls.

"Hard to say." Nico sighed, and I heard the squeak of a chair. I imagined the big guy leaning back in an oversize leather chair, his long hair clean and tied in a ponytail, a diamond in one earlobe, his biker boots propped on the desk.

"Could she be connected to the goons in the alley?"

"It's possible."

"Screw her then."

"Five mill's a lot of moolah, kid."

"No," I said. "But don't tell my sister."

I hung up and turned back to the diary. I pulled my new laptop across the duvet and tapped into various language dictionaries. I needed to translate more of the diary entries, clarify the French, and get a handle on the German. My Chinese was hopeless. I once asked a waiter in Beijing how he was doing and ordered horse by accident. When I sleepily dropped the diary on my nose for the second time, about

4:00 A.M., I carefully wrapped it in the scarf and stashed it back in its hiding place. Then I gave in to sleep.

The next day, a Friday, I avoided the diary. I needed to let my thoughts settle. I held morning classes and ran errands all afternoon. Outside, the world was gloomy and overcast. There was still snow on the ground. That evening, just before bed, I went downstairs to the yoga studio, moved the table aside, and gently wiggled the bricks loose. Curious Bella joined me. She rose up on two legs and poked her head in the hole. I pushed her away with a smile and reached inside.

The diary was gone.

CHAPTER 11

THE EIGHT SIDES OF LOVE

HERE'S WHAT I REMEMBER of the moments after discovering the diary had disappeared: nothing.

Apparently, though, I fled from the house and ran through the streets of Gabriel's Garden in my nightwear—no coat, gloves, or hat. Driving down Maple Lane, Jorn saw me, pulled over, and gave chase on foot. When I reached my parents' house, I flung open the door and collapsed into my mother's arms.

"I lost it!" I cried. "I lost it!"

Evie held me and petted my hair and made soothing sounds. She didn't ask questions. That's not her style. Evie always waits for answers to come to her.

When Jorn came clomping through the open door after me, he was breathing heavily and limping. "Christ, Maya, I've been yelling your name for three blocks," Jorn panted, bending at the waist and gulping air. "What's wrong?"

Larry clattered down the stairs, tennis shoes thumping. "What's going on? Why is Maya crying? Evie?"

"Come," Evie said, tucking me under her arm and leading me into the living room. She settled me on the sofa, her arm still around me, and I leaned into her. She wrapped an afghan around me.

"The diary," I whispered. "It's gone."

Jorn straightened. "What?"

Larry closed the front door, then sank into one of the two easy chairs facing the sofa. Jorn gingerly lowered himself into the other one. Larry's cell phone rang, but he ignored it. Upstairs, we heard the chimes of Evie's phone. No one moved.

I admit that sometimes, when in stress, I run home to mother. There is no place in Gabriel's Garden, in the whole world, like Evie and Larry's home. Designed by Evie, it is a modern octagon sitting on a circle of fieldstone. It is built according to the precise measurements of sacred geometry, a basilica of balance and integration. From the Chinese to the makers of the native medicine wheel, this shape has represented the mountain, the mother, and the movement of the cycles of life.

Although fascinated by numbers, I am not a serious student of sacred mathematics like Evie. But I believe in the oneness of the universe, in trusting in the patterns of nature that appear over and over again from the tiniest seed to the greatest star systems. And I believed Evie had created something special here. In Evie's house, I always felt better.

Larry leaned forward and said, "Tell us what happened, baby."

I told them about the new offer to make me a millionaire, five times over, and finding the diary gone. I didn't mention that I had read the entire diary. The fewer people who knew what was in the diary the better. I didn't want to burden my parents or tempt the reporter's instincts in Jorn.

"Tum entrusted the diary to me. I was supposed to protect it. I'm the keeper now." I pulled the afghan closer. "How could I have been so careless?" This guilt was immense. Even beyond the healing of chocolate.

"Whatever happened, it was not your fault." Evie stroked my hair from my face with her incredibly soft hands. Hand lotion was my mother's guilty pleasure. I smelled lavender. I closed my eyes for a moment and leaned my cheek into her palm. She laid her forehead against mine and whispered, "You are the keeper. You will get the diary back."

I sighed, and she kissed my forehead.

That's when Heart and Sadie burst in. "What's going on? Merlin just told me Maya was running around town like a crazy woman. And no one's answering the phone around here."

"Someone stole the diary," Evie said.

Heart's eyes grew round then she pumped her fist. "Yes!" She grabbed Sadie and whirled her around in a circle. Sadie laughed. Heart put her down and turned to us, all smiles. "This is great! Fantastic!"

Sadie crawled up on the sofa and leaned her colt-like body against me. "Why aren't you happy, Maya?"

"I lost something important."

Her face was close to mine, all big blue eyes like her father's and honey blonde hair like her mother's. While Heart's hair is straight and orderly, Sadie's hair is a riot of long curls, again David's influence. She edged closer until our faces were practically touching and gave me a butterfly kiss, long eyelashes fluttering against my cheek, our special offer of comfort to each other.

A joyous Heart couldn't wait to get Sadie home and share the good news with David. After she and Sadie left, we all piled into Larry's car, me wearing Evie's favorite purple jacket. Larry dropped Jorn off at his Jeep. Jorn said he'd meet us at my house.

"You don't have to," I told Jorn.

"It's more fun than writing up the zoning commission meeting."

I was too upset to argue. When we reached my house, the door was unlocked, just the way I'd left it.

As we entered, Larry asked, "Has this been unlocked all day?"

"Probably," I whispered, reaching down and lifting Bella into my arms.

My father sighed. Even after the break-in, it was difficult for me to break old habits. No one ever locked their doors in Whispering Spirit. In fact, many buildings didn't even have locks.

Evie patted Larry's arm, a calming gesture. "Weren't you going to take measurements for a security system? Two times is really too much, Larry."

My mother had experience distracting my father. "Right. Measurements," he said, pulling a tape measure from his pocket. A mission. Larry was good at missions.

Evie threaded her arm through mine and guided me into the yoga studio. "Let's sit." We sat cross-legged on my yoga mat and watched Larry commandeer Jorn to hold one end of the tape measure as he measured windows and mumbled numbers, filing them away in his memory drawers. Larry never wrote anything down.

Suddenly, Larry stopped as if struck by an idea. "Who knew how to find the diary? You said the diary was hidden."

"Yes."

Jorn and Larry exchanged looks. "Show us exactly," Larry said.

I hesitated, looking at Jorn. He flung up his arms in exasperation. "I swear I won't reveal your secret hidey-hole, Maya."

I shifted the table to the left of my yoga mat, jostling the Buddha, and removed the loose bricks. Hunkered before the hole, I motioned like a model in a car show. "There."

Larry walked over, studied the hole for a moment, poked his arm inside, then walked back to the middle of the room and slowly turned in a circle. Still sitting in lotus on my mat and with Bella now curled in her lap, Evie watched him. On his second revolution, Larry stopped and pointed to a spot near the opposite corner. "Grab me a chair," he instructed Jorn.

Jorn returned with a chair from the front office. Larry placed it against the wall and climbed up. He peered closely at what seemed to be a dirty spot on the wall.

"What is it?" Jorn asked.

Larry took out his Swiss Army knife and gouged a hole in the wall. He pried out a small object, then jumped down from the chair. He held the object up to the light. "It's a camera."

Evie's hand paused in stroking Bella.

"A camera?" I slowly stood and walked over to my father.

"Big Brother got here before me," Larry said. "It's pointed right at the front of the room, at your mat."

"Someone's been watching me?"

"They must have seen you hiding the diary one day and came back for it when you were out of the house," Jorn said.

Evie continued petting. "I suspect your first burglary wasn't just a break-in. When they couldn't find the diary, they installed the camera."

"Do you think there are more?" I asked, feeling ill at the thought of strange eyes spying on me.

While Jorn and Larry searched, I paced, chanting quietly to myself. I could feel Evie's reassuring presence. I don't recall ever having seen Evie lose it. She fought tension with relaxation; fear with positivity; distress with calm.

They found one other camera. This one was upstairs, positioned to see the entire living room and kitchen.

As everyone left, Larry taking the cameras with him and promising to be back tomorrow morning with a decent security system, Evie hugged me. "Don't worry."

I smiled and kissed her cheek.

Jorn lingered.

"You are *not* putting this in your stupid newspaper," I said.

Pulling on a knitted hat and fleece gloves, he said, "I've never met a woman who gets in as much trouble as you do."

CHAPTER 12

LADIES' DAY

WHEN YOU LOSE A book that people have died for, you do not get out of bed—for days. You feed the cat and make yourself a piece of cinnamon toast every once in a while. You cancel yoga classes due to "illness." You hide. You ignore Jorn banging at the door and e-mails from your family until one day your sister lets herself into your home with the key that was supposed to be for emergencies only. On that morning, your cat is patting your head incessantly, and you try to burrow deeper under the covers but you can't. Someone has ripped the covers from you. You can growl and threaten, but you know, when you open one eye, that you'll see *her* standing at the bottom of the bed. Heart.

"You need a haircut," she said, frowning at me. "It gets lifeless if you don't keep the ends trimmed."

I twisted my hair back so she couldn't see it.

"I can do it," my sister offered.

I trusted my sister with dye but not scissors. She was not a skilled stylist. She got caught up in obsessive loops, trying to "even up" one side or another. If I let a scissor-happy Heart near my hair, I was likely to end up with no hair at all.

Heart patted her shoulder-length perfect page boy—so shining and full of life. "Or," she continued, "we could drive into The Cities and have a ladies' day."

I sat up with a start. "Not a ladies' day!" I moaned.

Heart loved being pampered at a day spa called Colette's on Nicollet Mall. I, on the other hand, hated being smeared with goo, scrubbed with salt, and wrapped in seaweed tighter than a tamale. I could tolerate the massage with mango and cocoa butter afterward, but still, it was a hell of a way to hydrate, exfoliate, and restore my glow.

"From the looks of you, we're going to need the full treatment: facial, eyebrows, manis, pedis."

"And henna tattoos." I piped in. "Just a single rose on your shoulder. Something small and tasteful."

"No, I'm not letting some crazy woman dye my skin. Stop trying to distract me." She sniffed the air and made a face. "Shower. Now." When Heart decides she knows what's good for me, she is immovable.

I looked to Bella for sympathy, but she just made three circles and settled in a curl on my pillow, the cat equivalent of a shrug.

As I trudged out of the bedroom, showered and wearing the clothes Heart had laid out for me, she shoved a travel cup of tea and a piece of toast in my hand. "You don't have any food," she said. It had been a week since the diary was stolen, since I'd left the house.

"You don't have to do this, Heart," I said.

"What are sisters for?" She gave me a wicked grin and pushed me toward the door.

I hollered good-bye to the traitorous cat who didn't even leave my warm bed to walk us to the door, and we were off. Heart drove. I sat in the passenger seat of her Honda Civic Hybrid and pouted. Heart, who dealt with an eight-year-old on a regular basis, let my sullenness slide off her like Jello on a warm plate. We passed huge semis as if they were standing still; snow-covered fields blurred in the window. Sooner than we ought to have been, we were on Hennepin Avenue, driving past the Walker Sculpture Garden. It was the first week of April and still only twenty-eight degrees. No flowers bloomed in the garden. No water misted the air from the fountain-sculpture of a giant cherry resting in a spoon. Heart flitted through lanes, and soon we were in downtown Minneapolis on Nicollet Mall.

We spent two hours and several hundred dollars bringing out our inner beauty at Colette's. Heart insisted on paying. "You know," I told Heart as we left the spa, "we could have saved a ton of money by just doing a little yoga. Yoga gives good glow."

"I don't do yoga," she said. That didn't stop me from trying to get her to the occasional class. To be frank, Heart can be tense, like wired-on-a-gallon-of-caffeine, screaming-banshee edgy, when she's feeling overwhelmed by work or family or things that don't quite fit her world-view. Yoga and meditation, however, were remnants of our life at the Whispering Spirit Farm, a time Heart wanted to forget.

"Wasn't that seaweed wrap refreshing?" she asked, steering me down the street.

"It smelled fishy." I sniffed my arm. "Do I smell fishy?"

"You shed about a million dead cells."

"Like getting a whole new body," I said.

"I really need to get David in there." Heart paused to look at a dress in a store window. "Poor man is having fits over his greenhouse."

"Why?" I asked, studying the dress. The midnight blue gown was strapless with a skirt big enough to hide five kids under. The mannequin, looking over her shoulder at a train of bows and ruching down the back, was lifting the front of the skirt and about to step through a gold trimmed mirror. On her feet were apple green high-top sneakers.

"Great dress," Heart sighed.

"Great shoes," I said.

We reached Montaldo's, one of Heart's favorite restaurants because it serves baskets of popovers. I'd never seen a pastry filled with so much air until I moved to Minnesota. They were heavenly. As I buttered a popover, I said, "So tell me about the greenhouses."

Heart leaned back, closed her eyes for a moment, and sank into popover bliss. Then she filled me in: plants withering for no reason, shrubs browning, no bugs that David could find.

"Soil seems nutritious," she said. "Climate control thermostat's working. It's driving him bats."

I hesitated to bring up the diary, but . . . "I know you

don't want me to say it," I smiled at the waiter who placed two salads in front of us.

"Then don't."

"There must be balance."

"Maya, the diary is gone. We don't have to deal with that cosmic crap anymore."

"Still, Merlin broke his arm—"

"Like any of us could *not* have seen that coming. He's an old man bouncing on a trampoline."

"He received a gift," I said.

"And you think he paid the price."

All through lunch, it hung between us. Karma comes from the Sanskrit for "action"; it is the belief that all actions lead to inevitable results, both good and bad. The thing is you never knew when the "reaction" to that action would appear in your life. Was the trouble in the greenhouse the result of the blooming tree in March, a tree full of life?

Heart shook her head, signed the credit card receipt, and tucked her card back in her wallet. "I'm not letting you undo three hundred dollars of spa work. The plants will recover. David will be okay. Period." Cosmic payback was a bitch, and Heart was afraid to admit it.

I glanced out the window, spying a woman in pink on the sidewalk across the street in front of the Mary Tyler Moore statue. It was Sasha, and she was arguing with a man. He was big, in a well-tailored black woolen overcoat, no hat or gloves. "Look at that," I said, motioning to the window.

"Is that Julia's sister?" Heart asked.

I nodded, unable to take my eyes off the pair.

"Do you think she needs help?" Heart asked, considering

the giant who was leaning over Sasha. It was like watching a Transformer square off with a small Scandinavian doll in a heavily embroidered fuchsia coat and matching high-heel suede boots. And the Transformer was losing.

"I think she can handle him," I said, watching Sasha poke the guy in the chest. He dropped his head and stopped talking, which was good, because Sasha had plenty to say. She reamed him as passing shoppers and downtown workers jostled them. Finally, she flung up her hands and stalked away.

The man stood, for a moment, head hanging. Then he looked up at Mary, the one "who can turn the world on with her smile." She is flinging her beret into the air with happy abandon, just like in the television show.

The man looked both ways then kicked the statue.

CHAPTER 13

MEDITATION MARATHON

I AWOKE, GASPING, FIGHTING OFF the tangled arms of the bedcovers. The dream gnawed at the edges of my mind. Sitting up, I peered into the darkness, as if the haze of the dream would clear if only I could focus. I felt a hand on my arm. No, a paw. Bella was either telling me to go back to sleep or she was hungry.

I drew my knees up and held on. I struggled to remember the dream. I was running through a forest of weeping willows, their feathery fingers reaching for me. Attached to the waving fronds, like Christmas ornaments, were geometric shapes. Red cubes, blue spheres, black tetrahedrons, gold pyramids. Every time one of the shapes touched my skin, it burned. I held my arms close, trying to dodge the shapes, and then I burst from the trees and skidded to a stop—at the edge of a waterfall. I looked back at the trees and their nasty mathematics. I couldn't go back through them, but I couldn't go over the falls either. I was frozen in fear.

My room came back into focus. There was nothing but darkness. I pulled Bella into my arms and cradled her under my chin.

"Tum," I whispered.

I felt I knew something but couldn't pull it to the surface. Bits from the Down Dog Diary swam through my head. Once I had almost copied the journal, even had the first page on the scanner. But something stopped me. For some reason, it didn't feel right to transfer the contents of the diary to any other medium.

"Silly huh, Bella? Like there was some deep, dark magic that would be transferred via computer cables to an unsuspecting world." I sighed. "I know, that's a plot line from *Buffy*. I've got to start watching more documentaries." Bella flexed her claws in reply.

But now the diary was gone, and I had nothing.

A sentence from the diary came to mind: *Move the heart first.*

Abruptly, I set Bella on the bed and got dressed. On the way through the kitchen, I made a fist and banged the top of the automatic cat feeder in just the right spot. An unscheduled helping of cat food spewed into the bowl. Bella leapt on it. I hoped she never learned that trick. There would be no living with Bella if she could outsmart the timer.

I made a cup of tea, ate a slice of cinnamon toast, and licked a large gob of peanut butter from a spoon. Then, fortified, I walked down the stairs and into the yoga studio. I settled on my mat, legs in lotus, palms up; closed my eyes; and breathed.

Hours passed. I waited.

Someone entered the studio. I felt a presence. Without opening my eyes, I said, "Not now, Jorn."

"When?" he asked.

"Later," I said.

More hours passed. Once, in the ashram with Guru Bobastani, I sat in meditation for thirteen hours. For more than five thousand years, men and women have practiced yoga in order to be strong enough to sit in meditation. That is the purpose of yoga. It was never meant to compete with forty minutes on a Stairmaster. You can't strip the spirituality out of yoga. It always seeks the union of spirit, mind, and body.

As I slipped deeper into meditation, I heard buzzing. Whispers. Then the buzzing again. I remained in lotus, no longer feeling my body, as my mind fell back into the buzzing like a body into a lake, arms stretched wide, eyes closed, lips smiling, sinking down to the quiet bottom. And there I stayed.

When I finally surfaced, the first thing I saw was Jorn, across the room, sitting on the floor, his back against the wall. He was watching me.

"What are you doing here?" I asked, my voice raspy.

"I thought you might start levitating," he said. "I didn't want to miss it."

"I heard whispers."

"That was your mother."

"You called my mother?"

He checked his watch. "You haven't moved for five-and-a half hours. At least, that I know of. Who knows how long you were 'om-ing out' before I got here?" Jorn rubbed his knees. "I don't know how you can take it."

"Years of practice," I said.

"Evie said you were okay. Obviously, she's seen this kind of weird behavior before."

"Of course, I'm all right," I said. "Just working on some things." I flipped over onto my hands and knees and moved through a few Cats and Cows, poses for limbering the spine. Bella came trotting in and butted me with her head. I sank into Child's Pose, my legs curled under me, my forehead on the mat, and sighed.

"Working on what?" Jorn asked.

Without lifting my head, I mumbled into the mat, "My next step."

"You mean about the diary?"

I pushed into Down Dog, felt that delicious relaxation ripple through my body, then stepped to my hands and swept up to standing. Hands held in Prayer Pose, I bowed my head in *namaste* then strode across the room. I looked down at Jorn with a smile and offered a hand up. "Yes," I said.

When we entered the kitchen, the oven was on warm and something smelled heavenly. Evie had left vegetarian lasagna and garlic bread. My mother knew how hungry I'd be after a marathon meditation session. I invited Jorn to join me. We ate in silence at first. The transition from the meditative world to the concrete world can be like those first few moments after taking off roller-skates. You have to remember what the nonrolling world feels like. Jorn kept eyeing me, waiting for me to speak. Finally, I reached for my second slice of garlic toast and said, "One of the last entries in the diary was a message from Tum to me. He told me to trust."

Jorn's forehead wrinkled. "Trust whom?"

I shrugged. "This whole situation has a bad vibe, a terrible energy." Spicy pasta slid across my tongue. "But I'm the keeper."

Jorn stopped, his fork in mid-air, and stared at me. He set the fork down.

"You're going after the diary," he said.

"Who else is there?"

"Alone."

I seldom ask for help from anyone other than my family. I figure I was put on this cosmic roller coaster to hang on, ride it out, and keep the other riders from flying off, if I can. Yet, for some reason, the diary and Jorn were mixed up in my feelings. He was meant to help me; I just knew it. And I always act on my intuition. Sometimes we are the teacher, and sometimes we are the student. In this case, I didn't know which of us was which.

"Unless you want in." I gave him a long look.

The silence that greeted my offer was nearly a solid thing. Just when I thought he was going to laugh me off, one eyebrow quirked and a gleam of interest streaked across his eyes. One dimple appeared.

He leaned back in his chair, crossed his arms over his

chest, and pretended to be indifferent. "Help you find the diary," he said.

"That's the plan."

"Partners."

"I'd be the head partner, of course," I said.

Jorn's lips twitched. "Could it be dangerous?"

"Most likely."

He gave it a long thought. "All right," he finally said, picking up his fork and returning to his lasagna. "But I don't do vibes."

As we were finishing our meal, my phone rang. I snatched it up and saw that I had seven messages, all of them from Nico. And here he was, calling again.

"Where the hell have you been?" Nico growled when I answered.

"Meditating."

"All day? You people are so strange."

"What's up?" I asked.

"We've got a situation, and I'm ready to tear the State of New Mexico a new one."

"Breathe, Nico."

"Don't try to calm me. I enjoy righteous anger."

"What happened?" I asked, putting Nico on speakerphone. Jorn leaned forward. He patted his coat pocket and pulled out a small black notebook and pen.

"I've been fucked by every official channel in the state. They cremated Tum, what was left of him, without my authority. Then they lost the fucking ashes. Can you believe that?"

"Oh no."

"Don't worry. I finally tracked them down in some pencil pusher's office. Scared the shit out of that little guy. He'll never lose one of my friend's remains again."

"So you have them now?"

"Scattered them on his mountain at sunset, just like he wanted."

"I should have been there with you."

"Tum wasn't one for ceremony."

"No," I agreed. Still, I was ashamed that I had never even thought of how best to say good-bye to Tum. I had been raised better than that. When someone died in Whispering Spirit, we all paid our respects. Words were said. The individual's goodness was remembered.

I couldn't face saying good-bye, and now, I'd lost my chance.

With guilt in my voice, I said, "I lost the diary, Nico."

"Lost it? How the hell—"

"Actually, it was stolen."

"Tell me what happened."

So I did.

When I finished, Nico said, "Makes sense with all the weird shit going on."

"You mean the lost ashes?"

"They weren't the only thing misplaced. I wanted a copy of the autopsy report. That mysteriously disappeared, too. As did the coroner, that two-bit, rat-faced . . ."

"Nico," I interrupted.

"I know, I know, breathe."

"Why did you want to see the autopsy report?"

"Because it didn't feel right. I wanted to know how Tum died. We rode together, man. He was my brother."

"And, there's all this curiosity about the diary."

"That, too. So I went hunting. The coroner took a sudden vacation. To Hawaii. When I found that son of a bitch, I nearly shoved a flaming drink up his ass."

"I don't get it," I said.

"He was paid to get lost for a while and to bury the report."

"Why? What was in it?"

A sad sigh issued from the phone. "Tum was shot, Maya."

"No," I moaned.

"Point blank in the head."

I looked at Jorn, and he looked at me. Then he began scribbling in his notebook.

I couldn't believe it. Tum was murdered.

He had changed his ways. He had left the violent life. He had planned to go out of this world in a quiet way: happy, ready. Instead, he had been ripped from this existence. I closed my eyes as sorrow swept over me.

"And that's not all, Maya," Nico continued. "The fire marshal's now calling it arson. One of the firemen told me they found Tum's body tied to a chair. He didn't have a chance, those motherfuckers."

Long after Jorn left, I paced around the studio, Bella trailing in my wake. Nico suspected Tum had been tortured, probably for the location of the diary. "He wouldn't have told them shit, Maya," Nico reassured me. I knew he was right.

I thought of the last time I had visited Tum, back in August. He had been so proud of the kiva he had just completed next to his house. We sat together in the circular pit on the stone bench that ran around the walls. It was a small personal kiva, maybe five people at most could meditate in it at one time. We had to climb down into the chamber using a ladder made of logs. There was no roof.

"To be a true kiva, I should enclose it. A sacred room," he said. "But I like the sky, you know?"

I leaned back and absorbed the warmth of the sun-heated stone walls. Tum's mountainside hugged me. "It feels good," I told him. "Right."

That made Tum smile. Then we closed our eyes and christened Tum's kiva with its first meditation. We sat there until night came and the stars joined us.

Now that he was gone, the kiva was mine. I would go back there someday and say a proper good-bye.

But now there was work to do.

I pulled out the ladder and hammered a hook in the ceiling in the corner of the studio. Then, I dragged out my old punching bag and hung it.

It was time to train again.

CHAPTER 14

WALTZING WITH MATILDA

I CIRCLED THE BODY BAG, jabbing, hearing Tum's words in my head. "Focus on speed, movement, balance. Not power." My wrapped fists ached. I swiped my forearm across my sweaty face without missing a punch, flowing into another drill. I whirled and kicked, followed it with a jab and a hard straight punch. The punching bag wobbled. I practiced the combination again and again.

Who paid the coroner? Punch. So far, Nico was coming up empty. Jorn had tapped some of his newspaper cronies in the Southwest, but they were no help. Jab. We needed to slide into some bank accounts and take a look around. It sounded like a job for Larry. Side kick.

I stopped and hugged the swinging bag. When my pulse settled, I lifted the bag from the hook and stored it in the closet. An hour later, I stepped into my parents' house and shouted, "Hello, anybody home?"

My father yelled, "Up here."

I took the stairs to the second-floor office where my father sat in the center of a circle of computer monitors. A web of cables spun out of power strips. The custom-made, C-shaped computer desk, which held devices of various ages, makes, models, and purposes, formed an electronic embrace around Larry. Every screen glowed in the dark room, and Larry was rolling in his office chair from one to another. A conductor pulling a symphony of information from cyberspace. Eventually, he noticed me, spun around, and smiled. I crossed the room and pecked his cheek.

"Whatcha need?" he asked.

"I want to trace some money."

"Your credit cards?"

"Not my money. Someone else's."

"Ahh," Larry nodded, his silver ponytail bobbing. "Even better." He grabbed another rolling chair and spun it my way. "Give me the back story." I sat and told him about Tum's murder, the arson, the coroner sipping flaming drinks in Maui.

"I want to know who paid off the coroner."

Larry leaned back and listened, arms folded across his chest and a foot propped on his knee. He wore the ubiquitous tennis shoes. The eternal California boy tackled slippery Minnesota snowbanks in worn sneakers.

"This is a job for Matilda," he said. Matilda was one of

Larry's computers. "She loves the financial digging. She gets an account number in her bytes, and she'll track it to the ends of the earth."

He swung around and began tapping on a keyboard, presumably Matilda's. "It may take a while. Matilda is one thorough gal."

"No problem," I said, but my father was no longer listening. He was staring with child-like fascination at the screen as numbers and code streamed by, swishing through digital highways and canyons. I was forgotten. My father was sixty-two years old, except when he was in this room.

CHAPTER 15

A BROKEN INNOCENCE

B Y THE TIME I left Larry, it was nearly four o'clock in the afternoon. The days were longer, now that it was April, and there was plenty of light. It was an easy mile walk to my house plus an extra mile if I took the route around the lake. I always opted for the lake when I had time.

As I turned onto the lake loop, I met Alice Dunkirk. Alice walked everywhere with a sturdy stride and swinging arms. She was trim even after giving birth to seven children, now scattered from the Twin Cities to Seattle. On holidays, Alice's kids and their families filled her house to bulging. Alice baked and stepped over bodies in sleeping bags on the den floor. She let the grandchildren get away with stuff her kids never dared try. When she said her morning prayers, it took half an hour to cover everyone. Today she wore a coral jogging suit with a down vest and gloves.

"Still a nip in the air," Alice said.

"Yup," I said, picking up the pace to keep up with her.

Alice wasn't much for idle chit-chat. So we walked in companionable silence along the unpaved trail, still soft and muddy in some places from the melting snow. The lake was thawed in several spots, and I squinted into the water diamonds glistening in the low sun. The red-winged blackbirds were back from their winter vacation, and their conk-la-ree calls echoed across the icy water. I was smiling at them when I heard it.

A sob.

I placed a hand on Alice's arm, stopping her in mid-stride. She looked at me. "What?"

More sobbing.

This time Alice heard it as well. She snapped her mouth shut and immediately began scanning the woods around us. It sounded like a child. We slowly and quietly turned in circles, searching the surrounding area. The trees were just budding, and the underbrush was still sparse. We should be able to see the child.

Suddenly, Alice tapped my shoulder and pointed. I turned around and saw her.

Olivia.

She was huddled on the ground against a log about forty feet off the trail. Alice and I crashed up the slope through the leaves and brush. Olivia, hair tangled and jacket ripped at the shoulder, twitched in surprise when we reached her.

Her right cheek was violently red, and there was a scrape on her chin.

"Olivia, what happened?" I asked in a quiet voice.

She shook her head and began sobbing again. Alice draped an arm over Olivia's shaking shoulders and pulled her close. Our eyes met over Olivia's head.

"Let's get you out of here," Alice whispered to Olivia. "We're not far from my house. We'll go there and get you fixed up, dear. Good as new."

Together we helped Olivia to her feet and back to the trail. It was slow going; Olivia was limping. But in fifteen minutes, we were on Alice's porch, and she was unlocking the door to her two-story Colonial home. She guided us into an immaculate living room—a study in pastels, lush swags atop the windows, and silky fabric stretched over delicate French Provencal furniture. I glanced at our muddy boots in dismay. Olivia and I automatically toed off our boots. Even distress could not supersede some habits in Minnesota.

"Now, you sit right here," Alice said, settling Olivia onto the sofa. She unzipped her down vest and flung it on a nearby chair. "I'm going to heat some milk for hot chocolate and get the first aid kit."

Olivia had stopped crying on the way to Alice's house. Now she sat in silence, head bent, staring at her dirty hands and torn fingernails. I sat beside her, not touching her. I leaned closer and whispered, "Please, Olivia, talk to me."

Olivia's glance skittered off me, and she shook her head. The fingers of one hand began tapping as if typing some invisible text on her leg.

Alice breezed into the room and sat down on the other side of Olivia. "Here we are," she said. She pulled several antiseptic wipes from a box and began gently cleaning Olivia's face and hands. Olivia let herself be cared for, sitting perfectly still, as Alice swept away the dirt and blood and administered healing cream. All the while, Alice told stories of her own children and their many mishaps: scraped knees, broken arms, cut heads. Such a clumsy bunch, she said with a laugh. Finally, with a kiss to the forehead, Alice finished and left to get drinks. She returned with three mugs of hot chocolate on a tray, which she placed on the coffee table. She handed Olivia one mug and me another. Both were piled with miniature marshmallows.

Taking her place again on the other side of Olivia, Alice took a sip from her drink, which had no marshmallows, and said, "Now, Olivia dear, it is time to spill the beans." Florence Nightingale had been replaced by Mother Superior.

Olivia looked at her in panic. Her leg began a jittery beat.

"We have to know what happened to make it better," Alice said.

"No one can make it better," Olivia whispered.

My heart clutched. *Please, Spirit, not that.* I placed my hand to calm the pulsing leg just as I would do in yoga class.

Alice continued in a quiet but stern voice, a voice with experience in drawing information from unhelpful young sources. "How were you hurt, Olivia?"

Olivia shook her head.

Alice kept at her. "You have to tell us everything that happened, even if it's hard."

Olivia heaved a big sigh. We watched her. In a shaky voice,

her eyes beginning to water, she said, "They jumped me. Three guys—boys. One was really big. I fought and ran, but they caught me."

Alice and I waited.

"They caught me. I couldn't see their faces; they wore ski masks." She wouldn't look at me. "I fought. But they punched me in the face," Olivia said in a little girl voice. "In the face!"

You never forget the first punch to the face. The unexpectedness of it. The pain.

"They hit me," Olivia said, "and stole my book bag."

Alice touched Olivia's arm, then stared into her eyes. This was the look of a mother who had threatened to march wayward children to the confessional in the Catholic Church down the street unless they revealed all. "You were mugged?" She paused. "And nothing else?

Finally, signs of the old Olivia appeared. The spine straightened. The leg had begun tapping again. She rolled her eyes. "I was robbed. That's all. Isn't that bad enough?"

"We just want to make sure of *all* the details, dear."

"You're positive it was boys?" I asked.

"Yeah. One had a pierced tongue. Please. Like that's bad."

Alice said, "We should report this to the police."

"No!" Olivia turned to me and grabbed my hand.

"Why?" I asked.

Suddenly, Olivia couldn't meet my eyes. She swerved toward Alice. "We don't have to tell the police. Or my parents. Do we?"

I knew then there was more to the story. Alice said, "We have to do the right thing, Olivia."

"But you can't!" Olivia wailed.

I shifted. "Olivia. This is serious. You were attacked. Your stuff was stolen."

"But they'll put me in jail," Olivia cried.

"You?" Alice was puzzled. "Dear, you were the victim. This was *not* your fault."

Olivia's fingers had begun their invisible typing again. The energy in the room had changed. I placed my hand over Olivia's and tried to imitate Alice's stern countenance. "What was in the book bag, Olivia?"

Olivia looked from me to Alice and back again. Her shoulders sank. She bit her lip and whispered, "Books, my phone, my computer." There was a long pause. "And your diary."

If a runaway car had crashed through the front windows of Alice's pretty living room and stopped within an inch of killing us all, I couldn't have been more surprised. I never even considered our teenage kleptomaniac. My head had been filled with thoughts of far more nefarious thieves, probably someone who hadn't grown up with a room full of Hello Kitty stuff.

"YOU took my diary?"

Olivia wouldn't look at me.

Now that the shock was settling out of my system, I wanted to be angry with Olivia. But it was hard to do. The energy from Olivia's guilt was thick in the room, and my heart went out to her. "Olivia, why?"

Olivia took a shaky breath. "You remember when you had the break-in? I saw the diary and your hiding place. And then, you never put that book down. Not even when you were talking to the police. Not the whole time we were cleaning up. I thought it must be really special. Like magic."

"You don't know what you're messing with, Olivia."

"I'm sorry, so sorry. But, well, when my prayer didn't come true, I thought . . ."

"What?"

"I thought there might be something in the book to help." Olivia looked down at her hands then back at me. "Maya, I really needed that wish."

Alice sighed. "Oh, Olivia, there is no such thing as magic. No book can grant you a wish. What we did in yoga class was just a silly game."

"Did your wish come true, Alice?" Olivia asked.

Alice the good Catholic would never admit to that.

Olivia persisted. "What did you wish, Alice?"

"If you must know, I wrote 'Bless my children.' Does that make you feel better?"

"Pretty lame wish," Olivia muttered.

"Why was your wish so important?" I asked Olivia.

She threw up her hands in disgust. "Because he is like the most beautiful thing ever and I can't even talk to him!"

Boy trouble. I should have guessed.

"I get all tangled up when he's around. And I just wanted to be really cool."

"So you wished for courage," I said.

"Dumb, I know," Olivia whispered.

"Not dumb," I said.

"But I couldn't understand anything in that book." Olivia was a brilliant kid who would someday probably discover something incredible. But no matter how advanced intellectually, she still had all the insecurities of a fifteen-year-old girl. She changed the streaks in her hair on a whim, considered her eyes too boring, and thought ninety pounds was grossly over-weight. "There were all these languages and weird stuff. Like who cares about some guy's grocery list? And then there were parts that were just plain gross. Was that stuff real?"

I was beginning to wonder that myself. "Olivia," I said, "when you opened the diary, what did you smell?"

Olivia wrinkled her nose. "Smell? Nothing. It didn't even smell like a book."

Alice cleared her throat. "Why is this book important?"

"A friend died and left it to me," I said.

Olivia shifted. "That's a dead guy's book? Eww."

Over Olivia's bent head, Alice and I shared grins. Then Alice said, "What are you going to tell your mother and father, Olivia?"

There was a warning in Alice's tone. I watched Olivia pick at the rip in her jeans, making it bigger. Finally, she sighed. "Okay, okay, I'll tell them everything."

"Don't mention the diary," I said. Alice and Olivia turned to me in surprise. "I'll get the book back."

This time I won the stare down with Mother Alice. Finally, she nodded, and Olivia breathed a sigh of relief.

While Alice drove Olivia home, I returned to the lake. I searched the woods until darkness began to creep up on me. Just as I was turning away to head home, I saw something purple stuffed in a hollowed out tree stump. I tugged it free. Olivia's book bag.

It was empty.

CHAPTER 16

PLAYING AND BEING PLAYED

UNTIL LARRY CAME UP with information on who paid off the coroner, my only clue was the boys. I stood in the high school parking lot on a Monday afternoon, watching teenagers pour out the doors, energy released, hormones uncapped. Earbuds and cigarettes were tugged from pockets and book bags. Engines began to rev. I ignored the girls, who were dressed in either shorts or jean skirts. Kids in Minnesota. Fifty degrees in mid-April was reason to start on your tan. Instead, I studied the boys, especially the groups of three. I had a feeling that Olivia's assailants with their pierced tongues and penchants for ski masks were the same ones who tortured Bella. I listened to such feelings.

When I saw them, I stayed perfectly still, leaning against my Subaru, arms crossed over my chest. When they saw me, there was a momentary hitch in their steps and then they were slouching toward me. They didn't stop, but they maintained eye contact and laughed as they passed. The one with the long blond curls and pale face was the leader. Wearing a leather jacket and a sneer, he walked slightly ahead of the other two. Snowboard Boy had on a knitted cap just like the day on the lake when he offered me the wet sack. His followers were the guy with the piercings and a lanky black kid shivering in a boy band T-shirt. Without his puffy parka, Pierced Boy was still massive, a white whale in a hoodie. What I could see of his unwashed hair was disgusting.

I knew in my heart that they had preyed on Olivia, just as they had preyed on Bella. The more I thought of Olivia's swollen and bruised face, the angrier I became. It was my fault she got hurt. I was responsible for the diary. I was the keeper. Heart had warned me. No good could come from having the diary in Gabriel's Garden.

Each day that week I stood in the parking lot. Maybe I couldn't touch them, but I could stalk them. On the second day, Snowboard Boy whispered, "How's the cat?" and his friends snickered as they passed. I stared at them in silence. On the third day, they made meowing sounds, and Snowboard Boy tapped his knitted cap in salute. Still I stared. By Friday, they weren't so talkative; they took another route off school property, looking over their shoulders at me. I watched until they were out of sight. I was wearing them down.

The following Monday I was back in front of the high

school, which was still buttoned up before the last bell. Today I planned to confront the boys. I was hoping one of them would break, fall to his knees, and confess. Who knew? I might have Tum's diary back by nightfall. An expectant quiet hovered over the school parking lot. Soon the afternoon would explode with self-absorbed teens, lovers who couldn't keep their hands or their tongues to themselves, and car engines growling to escape.

Into this silence glided Sebastian Winter in a silver BMW. He pulled up beside me, rolled down the window, and smiled at me. "Can I buy you a cup of coffee?" I tilted my head at him, trying to get a better look at his eyes. He had on sunglasses. He had become a regular at Monday yoga classes. Why was he still in Gabriel's Garden? David's crazy blooming tree was old news. Didn't he have another story to chase, an empire to run? Maybe this was my chance to learn more about the man Jorn hated. I decided the boys could wait.

"Sure," I said.

Sebastian leaned over and pushed open the passenger door of the BMW. I hesitated a moment, then got in, just as a bell sounded and life flooded the parking lot.

He drove to the Northern Lights coffee shop downtown. A bell tinkled when we entered the shop, and Hallie, the proprietor, looked up. "Hey, babe." She waved.

I nodded. "Hallie." I didn't need to study the chalkboard hung behind the counter. "Mint tea, please."

"You got it." She turned to Sebastian. "The usual, Mr. Winter?"

"As dark and strong as you can make it, Hallie." He gave

her a charming smile then winked at me. "Espresso. My addiction."

Although she talked like a New York cabbie, Hallie reminded me of many of the women I had known growing up: quick to smile and hug, adamant about serving only free-trade products, and a soft touch for every kid raising money for a school trip or new band uniforms.

Sebastian paid, and we took our drinks to a table by the window. He pulled the chair out for me, and I nodded my thanks. I took a sip of my tea and glanced up at the ceiling, which always filled me with a sense of rightness. A mural of the aurora borealis or northern lights stretched across the café's domed ceiling, curtains of green particles sweeping and swirling through a dark sky over a pine landscape outlined in pink and orange. Magnetic storms can lure auroras far from their polar homes during the equinoxes. According to Larry, the night I was conceived an aurora of amazing beauty danced above Tulum.

Sebastian pushed his black hair behind his ears and studied me. "You're a hard one to figure out, Maya Skye."

He'd flung his change on the table. I watched him select a quarter from the pile and begin rolling it over his knuckles and under his fingers, back and forth, weaving like a snake. It was a well-practiced move. The coin never slipped.

I pointed to the coin. "Are you a magician?"

Sebastian's lips curved, but he didn't stop. "You're the one with the tricks."

"How do you mean?" I asked.

"You have no footprint in the land of the interwebs, Maya." So Sebastian had been hitting some of Larry's digital walls.

"Surely, with all the investigative power at your disposal you could find something," I said with a tsk.

"Not what I wanted."

"And that was?"

We stared at each other for a moment. We were the only customers in Northern Lights. From a distance, we could have appeared to be lovers. But there at the table, the air was thick. Some would have found it uncomfortable; I didn't mind it. Then suddenly Sebastian smiled, and the air began to move again. "Just to find out more about my yoga teacher. I always make sure I know with whom I'm dealing."

"I bet you do."

"It never hurts to check credentials."

I shrugged. "Credentials are meaningless. Any kid with half-way decent hacker genes can manufacture them."

He studied me. "So true. Makes you wonder who you can trust in this world."

I leaned forward, plucked the quarter from Sebastian's busy fingers, blew on it, and made it disappear. He froze for a moment then looked at me more intently. I knocked on the table and opened my other hand. In it was the quarter. I presented it to him with a wink. He hesitated then took it carefully from my fingers.

"Personally," I said, "I judge people by their actions, not by the words on a computer screen." I picked up my cup and sipped. "Tell me why you and Jorn are enemies."

For a moment, I didn't think he was going to answer. He'd placed the quarter on the table in front him, apart from the pile of change. "Peter believes there is only one truth," he said, "while I see a world of many truths."

"A world of many truths." I mulled that over.

Sebastian leaned forward, warming to his subject. "Today anyone with a smartphone can be a reporter. My resources are legion."

"Once again, any kid . . ." I waved my hand. "That's not really reporting. Just spewing information. And you don't even know if it's true."

"Peter is a dinosaur in today's news world."

"Because he believes in research and fairness and checking facts instead of reporting by stopwatch."

"No one can control the news today so why try?"

I shook my head in sadness. "Still taking shortcuts, just like your college days."

"So, you've been talking to Peter."

"In yoga, the practice of *satya* or truth means choosing our words so they do the least harm. Your 'reporters' give little thought to that. You don't care what harm your broadcasts and websites do."

Sebastian dipped his head. "I give people what they want, Maya. Something to take them away from their dreary little lives, as my dear mother says."

I'd come across Madelyn Winter in my research of Winter Media. She married a hopeless and poor newspaperman who died early, leaving her to raise a young son and build a publishing dynasty alone. She was shrewd and ruthless, and many were shocked when, three years ago, she agreed to turn the reins of Winter Media over to her son.

I could imagine a young Sebastian playing sleight of hand tricks on his mother—"Pick one, Mother, pick one"— and she revealing his secret every time. She would have been tough on him. She would have wanted to make him into something more than his father was.

"Diversion," I said, nodding to the quarter he'd been finger rolling. "That's not news; that's entertainment."

Sebastian sat back with a laugh. "They're one and the same in today's world."

"I hear Edward R. Murrow rolling over in his grave."

"Peter is a newshound. He gets on a scent, and he won't let go of the story until it nearly kills him. Like it did in Afghanistan."

"What do you know about that?"

In expensive trousers, a soft open-collar shirt, and a brown tweed jacket, Sebastian looked the successful businessman on vacation. He flicked a piece of lint from his lapel. "I know he was betrayed, and he left his friend and photographer, Gasquet, behind." He paused. "You think you know Peter Jorn, but you don't."

I frowned. I didn't believe him. When it came to people, I relied on instincts, and I knew Jorn wouldn't abandon his photographer.

Sebastian continued, "Gasquet has yet to turn up."

"How do you know this?"

Sebastian watched me. "I make it my business to know these things."

"Sebastian, what are you really doing here?"

"Enjoying coffee with a beautiful woman."

"No, in Gabriel's Garden."

Sebastian picked up the quarter, flipped the coin in the air, caught it, and shoved it in his pocket. "I still have business here."

"Gabriel's Garden is a small fish," I said.

"But such a lovely one, all shiny and colorful. It has mysteries. I like a good mystery."

"Some puzzles can never be solved."

"Oh, I'll solve this one. I'm good at puzzles."

I thought of David's tree, which was still blooming—and had been for months—even though all the other trees had just started to leaf out. "I wouldn't bet on that."

Sebastian stiffened. I was looking at a man who didn't like to lose. I could imagine him stealing a story from a young reporter, a former roommate, supposedly his friend. Jorn said Sebastian played dirty but made it appear aboveboard. A sleight of hand. A knife in the back.

"You know," he said, "I'm beginning to like it here. Maybe I'll start my own newspaper. Compete with *The Independent*."

"Good luck with that. Gabriel's Garden doesn't need two papers."

"But I don't have to make money. *The Independent* does. Peter would go under in six months."

"That paper has been in his family for three generations," I lowered my voice, a hint of threat.

"I'd be doing him a favor. Peter doesn't really want to be saddled to this small backwater," Sebastian said.

"He seems to like it well enough," I said.

"He's bored. Peter Jorn seeks the truth in bandits' caves and politicians' offices, not zoning commission meetings and hotdish recipes."

I opened my mouth to tell Sebastian he was wrong when my phone chimed. I glanced at the screen. It was a text message from my father: *Matilda sends her love.*

"I've got to go," I said.

"So soon? I feel like we were just getting to know each other." He threw a five-dollar bill on top of the rest of the change on the table and escorted me out of Northern Lights. I glanced at my phone. I had just enough time to get to Larry's and then back to the studio for the Monday five o'clock class.

Sebastian walked me to the passenger side of the BMW. Just as he opened the door for me, Jorn pulled up and got out of his Jeep. He looked from me to Sebastian and back again. "Peter," Sebastian said with a big smile.

Jorn ignored Sebastian. He turned to me. "You need a ride?"

Sebastian said, "She has one."

The air between the two men bristled. We didn't have time for this. "Actually," I said, "I have something to discuss with Jorn before class. See you later at yoga, Sebastian?"

Sebastian's smile stayed on his face as he reluctantly stepped back. "Of course."

I climbed into Jorn's Jeep. Jorn stared at Sebastian a moment longer then joined me. I directed Jorn to drive to Larry's.

After three blocks of silence, Jorn asked, "Did you enjoy your tea?"

"Sebastian was pleasant company," I said.

"Sebastian is never pleasant."

"He's thinking about starting a newspaper here."

Jorn let out a bark. "He can try."

"You're not worried about the competition?"

"He's not interested in this little burg."

As we arrived at my parents' house, I said, "He keeps tabs on you. He knows about Afghanistan."

"He knows nothing," Jorn said, shutting off the motor.

JORN TOOK ONE LOOK at my father's office, and his eyes widened. Seeing Jorn's interest, a delighted Larry rolled around amid his computers, explaining what he was doing with this one and that one. Quickly, Jorn was on information overload, his eyes glazed, his mouth open. Finally, I interrupted my father, "Matilda, Larry, Matilda."

"Right, right." Larry scratched his head, then swung over to a monitor on his left. He tapped furiously and ended with a flourish. "So, Matilda has been digging her little heart out."

"Matilda?" Jorn whispered to me.

"The computer," I mumbled. He nodded. We stepped closer and peered at the numbers on the screen, columns of numbers, large amounts. It looked like a bank account.

"The medical examiner's?" I asked.

Larry nodded. "Accounts in the Caymans and Switzerland."

"I found out that much," Jorn said. "I just couldn't get into them."

"Matilda has her ways," Larry said with a gentle pat to Matilda's monitor. "Unusually large deposits made at the time of Tum's demise can be tracked to a London company. That company is buried in tunnels of other companies. But, Matilda found a holding company. Tiger Corp."

Jorn straightened. "Are you sure?"

Larry had no doubt in Matilda's abilities. "Positive."

"Why?" I turned to Jorn. "Do you know this company?"

"I know it."

Jorn refused to elaborate, so I thanked my father, gave him a hug, and left with Jorn.

Jorn dropped me off at my car, which was one of three still left in the school parking lot.

"Are you coming to class?" I asked, getting out of the Jeep.

"I wouldn't miss it for the world," he said.

CHAPTER 17

SHOPPING LIST: MORE SAGE

THE MONDAY YOGA CLASS started as all others, with Jorn on one side of the room and Sebastian on the other. Jorn was sweating in minutes, his shoulder and hip taking their sweet time loosening up. Sebastian, on the other hand, flowed through the practice like a prized student of Guru Bob. His breathing was even, deep, and calm. In a silk tank, his muscles gleamed. He wore loose-fitting pants and tied his hair back in a short ponytail. Instead of a rubber mat, he used an indigo handwoven Ashtanga yoga rug. It looked well used, an old friend, and it surprised me that Sebastian would be so sentimental as to drag his yoga rug around with him. I once commented on how lovely it was. Sebastian told me it was a gift from an Indian prince.

Merlin was back in class, his broken arm healed. I watched him carefully, suggesting the occasional alternative pose when he seemed to be having trouble. Sasha, with a bright pink yoga mat, was set up behind Jorn, as usual.

Jorn didn't own his own mat. He maintained he wouldn't need yoga long enough to make the investment so he just grabbed any mat from the pile when he came in, as did Julia, who often forgot to bring one of the three yoga mats in her hall closet. Alice always brought her own, a double-thick purple mat. The first time Alice came to class she asked if I sanitized the mats between classes. Apparently, Alice doesn't trust me.

I looked at the empty spot in front, to my right, the place where Olivia always practiced. It had been more than a week since the attack. When I called her, she said she couldn't come back to class yet.

"Maybe next Monday, Maya," Olivia said.

I knew she was embarrassed.

"Sure," I said. "When you're ready. But Olivia . . ."

"Yes?"

"I miss seeing that crazy mat of yours."

I think I heard her laugh. Olivia's mat was orange and red and covered in tropical flowers and vines. In one corner, she'd taken a black magic marker and drawn a tiny skull. It was so Olivia, a sweet kid trying hard to be tough.

As the final *om* dissolved into silence and students began rolling up their mats, I saw Jorn get up and walk across the room toward Sebastian. I immediately jumped to my feet and followed. Just as I reached the two men, I heard Jorn say, "You paid off the M.E."

My head whipped around to Sebastian. What had Sebastian to do with events in New Mexico?

Locked in a stare with Jorn, Sebastian said in a low voice. "I don't know what you are talking about."

"Tiger Corp.," Jorn said. "It's your company."

Arrogance flowed off Sebastian and iced the room. "I don't discuss my business with you, Peter."

I stepped up. "Is there a problem here?"

Jorn spared me a glance. "He's Tiger Corp. His company paid the New Mexico medical examiner to falsify the report on Tum's death."

My mind spun. "Sebastian?" I asked. "Is this true?"

"No."

"Liar," Jorn spat.

Sebastian stood remarkably still, composed, while Jorn was vibrating with anger. I glanced around the room. The other class members had paused in their preparations to leave and edged closer to us. Julia and Alice looked puzzled. Sasha had a grin on her face, the kind you see ringside.

Jorn said, "James Tumblethorne was an old man. A friend of Maya's. He was murdered."

Sebastian said, "My condolences."

"Nice act. You're never sorry, Sebastian."

"You, on the other hand," Sebastian said, with a smirk, "are smothering in regrets. Poor Gasquet, to hook up with a partner like you."

I sucked in a breath.

Jorn launched himself at Sebastian. I shouted for Jorn

to stop, but it was too late. The men were on the floor rolling around on Sebastian's yoga rug. Jorn landed a punch to Sebastian's right cheek. Sebastian only grunted, lifted both hands, and clapped Jorn's ears. Jorn fell off him, shaking his head, and, in an instant, Sebastian was on his feet. I recognized the stance immediately. Sebastian was a trained fighter. Jorn winced as he rolled to standing. He moved his shoulder, testing it, then put fists up to his face.

Jorn was a pugilist, while Sebastian was a mamba, fast-moving and deadly. He was playing with Jorn, striking a rib here, a thigh there. But Jorn was tenacious; he kept swinging, connecting more than I thought he would. Sebastian's opening came, and with a single blow, he opened up a cut in the corner of Jorn's eye. Everything after that seemed to happen in slow motion. A drop of blood fell to the studio floor. Jorn's weary hand swept across his face, his guard down. I saw the kick coming. Sebastian wouldn't pass up this opportunity. He slammed into Jorn's injured hip, and Jorn's leg buckled under him.

Jorn went down. I heard someone gasp.

I stepped between the two, just as Sebastian was going in for the finishing strike. I automatically blocked the punch that was headed for Jorn's swollen eye. Sebastian turned on me, fury mixed with shock.

"Enough!" I shouted. "Where do you think you are?"

Sebastian lifted a brow, and for a moment, I thought he was going to push me aside. Then he stepped back.

Jorn started to get up. "Maya, get out of the way."

I jabbed a finger at him. "You. Stay down."

I was disgusted with both of them. "This is a yoga studio. *My* studio. People come here for peace not brawling."

Turning back to Sebastian, I said, "You. Get out. This was your last class."

I imagine not many people threw Sebastian Winter out. His look turned glacial. He lowered his fists. "As you wish." Sebastian bent and grabbed his yoga rug. Slowly and carefully, he rolled it, never taking his eyes from mine. When he was finished, he gave me a salute and a cocky smile. "We'll see each other again."

After Sebastian departed, the other students gathered around Jorn.

"Are you all right, Peter?" asked Alice with a frown. Any minute now she was going to ask for my first-aid kit.

"It was a lucky punch," Merlin said.

"What were you two fighting about?" Julia asked. She'd grabbed a towel and was dabbing at the cut near Jorn's eye.

"That probably needs stitches," Alice said.

Sasha leaned against the wall, watching the others' ministrations. "My, my, your yoga classes are exciting, Maya."

"Glad we could entertain you, Sasha," Julia said.

"Oh, Julia, it was just a little altercation. Boys will be boys," Sasha said.

"Not in my studio," I glared at her.

I knelt next to Jorn and took the towel from Julia. After a rough swipe at his cheek, which made Jorn wince, I said, "I am so mad at you right now I can't think straight. Sebastian's not rehabbing, and he's trained in martial arts. Not to mention all the negative energy you've just smeared all over the place!"

Jorn grabbed the towel from me. "Excuse me, I had more on my mind than your precious energies. Like getting my ass kicked!" He groaned to his feet, and everyone faded back, leaving just Jorn and me in a silent face-off. From the corner of my eye, I saw Merlin and Alice turn to leave. Julia walked over and picked up her borrowed yoga mat; she grabbed Sasha's pink one and pushed it into her sister's arms. "But I want to watch," Sasha whined, as Julia shoved her toward the door.

Finally, we were alone.

"Sebastian's in this," Jorn said. "You know it, and I know it."

"Well, since you didn't beat a confession out of him, we'll have to find another way to get some answers."

"Is that a crack about my fighting skills?"

"You have skills?"

"He cheats. He always does."

I rolled my eyes. "Get out."

"You're throwing me out, too?" Jorn couldn't believe it. He stomped toward the door, holding the towel to his head. "You know, you could use some lessons in teamwork. A partner has your back. A partner takes your side. A partner offers you a lousy Band-Aid."

I STOOD IN THE center of the yoga studio, alone. I had never been a team player. Unlike Heart, I enjoyed being different. Evie and Larry raised us to think for ourselves and follow our hearts. My sister has always been cautious—she never leaps without looking. I, on the other hand, react and don't even slow down at the edge of the cliff.

I had not handled this well. I had driven away Sebastian Winter when I needed to keep him close to discover his connection to Tiger Corp. And I'd pushed Jorn away with my New Age excuses because I didn't want to face how much it hurt to see him bloody and beaten.

I sighed and walked to the closet. I needed to purify the studio before going to bed. I lit the bundle of sage. Praying, I walked to all four corners of the studio, pausing at each and pushing the smoke with my hand toward the corner. Once, I met an old Indian woman who said she could see the "dark spots" on a spirit-body, areas that needed healing or cleansing. Although I don't see such spots, I feel them. I feel the leftovers of violence, the taints of bad energy. Sage drives out the bad spirits, feelings, and influences. It also drives out Bella. As soon as I started the ceremony, the kitten scooted from the room. She stopped just outside the door, sank to the floor, dropped her muzzle between her paws, and watched me.

After sage comes cedar, same process, moving to all four corners. Prayers rise on the cedar smoke and are carried to the Creator. Cedar not only shows bad energies the road, but also invites good energies in. To bring in more good spirits and influences, I next burned the powerful sweetgrass, which I bought in a Native American store. Finally, I lit a candle and paced the perimeter of the studio, pushing its light into every corner. The native people of the Pacific Northwest Coast call this "lighting-up," and it never fails to "clear the air."

When I was satisfied the studio had been cleansed, Bella and I slowly climbed the stairs to my apartment. It was long past dinner. Dragging with exhaustion, I sliced an apple and thought, Tiger Corp. I should Google it, but not tonight. I pushed away from the kitchen counter, walked into my bedroom, and dropped my clothes. As I slid in between the sheets, I yawned. If I'm going to keep hanging out with Jorn, I'll need more sage.

CHAPTER 18

IT'S A JUNGLE OUT THERE— AND IN HERE

WHEN OUTNUMBERED, ALWAYS GO for the leader. This is the cut-off-the-head-of-the-snake strategy. When followers have no one to follow, they melt away. Besides, I wasn't interested in Pierced Boy or the boy band lover. I was going for Snowboard Boy, the one who wore knitted hats like an emblem and could afford expensive ski jackets.

I hadn't seen Jorn or Sebastian for a week. Neither came to Monday yoga class. I was back on the trail of the diary, alone, missing Jorn but not ready to admit it. It was a Wednesday afternoon, and I was following Snowboard Boy home from school. I fell back about a block; it wasn't hard to keep an eye on that swagger. I imagined this punk smacking Olivia. She was tiny, of delicate bone, defenseless. He was short but sturdy and oozed attitude with every step. I was going to enjoy this.

I stepped behind a tree as Snowboard Boy stopped in front of a large brick house. It had a white picket fence, I kid you not. I had expected the boy came from affluence but not this tidiness. The front yard was filled with gardens, all neatly prepared, orderly, weeded until they were bald. Tulips were painting the spring air with color. I bet his father was an executive in The Cities and his mother, from the looks of the flower beds, was a neat freak.

The boy opened the white gate and swaggered up the cobblestone walk. I was about to step out from behind my tree when the front door flew open and a small girl launched herself from the top porch step. She threw herself into the air, right into the boy's arms. He automatically caught her and drew her close.

"Mikey!" she giggled. "It's park time. You promised."

"No way. I can't be seen with a runt like you."

Obviously this was a running gag because the girl, who appeared to be about four and had long yellow curls just like her brother, pinched his ear. He pretended that it hurt. Still clutching his earlobe, she pulled his head closer and in a loud whisper said, "I got a new superpower today."

Mikey leaned back and stared her in the eye. "Yeah? What?"

"I can walk on the moon."

He set her down. "Show me."

She began sliding backwards down the cobblestone walk,

lifting her heels, swinging her arms. Mikey started laughing. "You're a kick, kid."

She grinned and threw herself at his legs. He looked down at her, smoothed her hair, and said, "Okay. The park. Only a half hour. Let me go tell Mom we're going."

The girl stopped him. "She's taking a nap."

Mikey crouched down to her level. "You okay?"

She nodded. "I did just what you said. I stayed in the house and made sure she ate lunch. And I hid the bottle so Daddy wouldn't see it. I covered her up and tucked Sparky in with her so she won't be by herself when she wakes up. I did good, right?"

Mikey rose and took her hand. "Yeah, you did good."

Then he led her to the park.

I followed them.

It was one of Gabriel's Garden's many little neighborhood green spaces with a playground and one tennis court. It was empty, and from the cover of a huge blue spruce, I watched him warn the girl to be careful on the slide and pretend to scare her as she came through the tube in the middle. He called her Lissa.

After several turns down the slide, Lissa decided she was thirsty and ran to the water fountain, which was too tall for her to reach. Mikey began to lift her, but she said, no, she wanted to do it herself. Mumbling something about her being "a pain," Mikey dropped down to his hands and knees so she could step on his back and use him as a footstool.

I waited until Lissa had jumped down and Mikey was pushing her on the swing before I strolled up.

"Hi, Mikey," I said.

The boy jumped. He glanced in my direction and tensed. He quickly shot a look toward his sister.

I kept my hands in my pockets and smiled at the girl. "You must be Mikey's sister. What's your name?"

"Lissa," she called, pumping her legs to the sky.

"Pretty name. Sounds like a dancer's name to me. I bet you're a dancer."

Lissa dragged her feet to slow down then popped out of the swing. She instantly began to moonwalk. I clapped and told her she rocked.

The whole time we were talking Mikey stood stiffly by my side. Finally, he stepped forward and said, "Liss, let me talk to the lady. Go climb something."

Lissa waved good-bye to me and began scaling a rope wall. She was dainty in a red jacket with cats and butterflies embroidered on the sleeve and wearing Velcro tennies not much longer than my outstretched palm. They had flashing lights in the soles.

Without taking his eyes off his sister, Mikey said in a low voice, "What do you want?"

We stood in the park, side by side, both appearing to be tenderly caring for a child daring the laws of gravity on a play set.

"I want the diary."

"Don't know what you're talking about."

"You broke into my home and took my stuff," I said.

"Prove it," he said.

"You attacked Olivia Chen."

Silence.

"You hit her."

More silence.

"I want the book you stole from Olivia and her other stuff."

"I got nothin' to say to you."

"Olivia can identify you," I said.

Mikey snorted with disbelief. "I wasn't there, remember?"

I waved at Lissa, and she laughed and waved back.

I said, "You think Lissa likes cat stories?"

The boy hunched his shoulders and turned to me. His eyes were cold and hard. "Stay away from her."

"Or what? You'll hit me, too?"

"I didn't hit . . ."

I cut him off. "I know a great story about a poor little kitten that nearly froze to death in a big, cold lake. I bet Sparky is a toy kitten."

"How'd you know . . ."

I hadn't known, really. I just had one of my feelings and followed it. "Your sister looks like a cat person," I said.

Mikey called out to Lissa not to climb too high. She gave him the thumbs up.

"I told you, I don't know anything."

"You don't want to mess with me, Mikey."

He wore that old sneer I'd come to know so well. "Yeah, you're a real bad ass, threatening a four-year-old."

"You have no idea," I said.

Watching Mikey with his sister, knowing what waited for them behind the white picket fence every day, I had to bluff. I knew I couldn't turn in Mikey and his pals, and I wouldn't be telling Lissa any sad cat stories. But Mikey didn't know that. He didn't know that I'd been raised on oatmeal sprinkled with live and let live. Whispering Spirit alumni seldom brought in the authorities. Old habits and all that. Still, I had to get the diary back.

"Start from the beginning," I prodded him. "Who paid you to rob me?"

"If I tell you, will you leave us alone?"

I nodded.

Lissa hung upside down, her knees clamped to a bar. "Look at me, Mikey."

"Great, Liss," he shouted. He gave her a thumbs up, and she returned the gesture, only in her inverted position, her thumbs pointed down. He sighed. "We weren't supposed to rob you; we were supposed to make it look good. Mess up the place. I don't know why. It was Hank's idea to take the stuff. He needed a new TV."

"Hank?"

"The guy with the pierced tongue."

"So that's when you planted the cameras?"

Mikey took a step back. "Whoa. We had nothing to do with any cameras. We're not like perverts or spies or anything."

So someone else came in after the boys and installed the cameras. I said, "But who hired you?"

"A voice on the phone. Money left in a paper bag on the bench by the lake. We got a hundred each for messing the place up. You know, you oughta lock your door."

"So I've been told."

I peered out over the park. It was a quiet spot, surrounded by houses. An asphalt path ran through it and off between the houses, a walking trail connecting this neighborhood to another one.

"Describe the voice. Accented?"

Mikey thought for a moment. "Not Southern or Minnesotan. But there was definitely something there. A man's voice."

"And did the same voice hire you to beat up Olivia Chen?"

Mikey ducked his head. This one bothered him. "We were just supposed to scare her. Grab the book bag. But she came out fighting, you know. She goes all crazy on us. Hank accidentally clocked her."

"An accident?" Disbelief in my voice.

"Yeah, he forgets he's like Hulk strong sometimes. And then she starts crying and shit. So we ran. The voice on the phone said to take some old book. We snatched the computer and phone to make it look like an ordinary mugging."

"Where's the book now?"

"We left it at the usual spot. The bench by the lake. We put the book in a paper bag and swapped it for the bag left for us. Our money. Two hundred each."

I closed my eyes in disappointment. When I opened them, Mikey was staring at me.

"Did you see who picked up the book?" I asked.

Mikey shook his head. "Didn't want to know."

I had hoped to scare Mikey into giving me a name or a description, but he didn't have one.

"Why?" I asked him. "Why did you do it? You obviously don't need the money."

Mikey looked away. He was uncomfortable. When he turned to me, the sneer was back. "Sometimes you just do shit." Our gazes locked, and I realized that I probably could never comprehend Snowboard Boy's life. I had never been so desperate to feel in control.

"Okay," I said. "Here's the deal. I don't care about my stuff. But Olivia is another matter. Give her back her computer and phone. I don't care if you walk up to her in school or leave it on her doorstep in the middle of the night."

"No way."

I waited him out, saw his sneer slide away in the face of my silence, watched the nerves set in. He glanced at his sister and back at me.

Finally, he said, "If we do this, we're square? You'll leave Lissa alone? You'll stop stalking us?"

I nodded. "And one more thing. Stop taking jobs from strange voices on the phone. Lissa deserves a better brother."

Mikey gazed at his sister for a moment. As I was walking away, Mikey called out, "How'd you know it was us? In the apartment?"

I turned and moonwalked backwards. "You put my cat in a bag, Mikey."

CHAPTER 19

ABANDONED WITH ARMADILLO

THE CROW AND BELLA stared at each other through the window pane, beak to nose. Bella sat on the bedroom window seat, riveted, still, except for the tiniest twitch of the tip of her tail. Suddenly, the crow pecked the glass near Bella's nose. She jumped, flipping backwards off the seat. I laughed. The crow turned to me. I stopped laughing. We watched each other for a moment, then it pecked the window twice, sharply.

I knew it was time to go to New Mexico.

Among Tum's many tattoos was a crow on his right shoulder. When I asked him about it, he said the crow is the keeper of magic. Some cultures believed the crow brought death and could shape-shift; others believed it created the world. When I was young, I thought Tum not only carried the mark of the crow but was a crow, a man transformed who had shape-shifted, recreating himself, from hell raiser to gentle giant.

Crows are highly intelligent and can be taught to count and communicate with humans. They remember the faces of people they do not like and, in Japan, have found a way to trick cars into opening nuts for them on the roadway.

When a crow comes to your door, pay attention.

I scooped up Bella from the floor and stroked her small head. "Crows are impossible to catch," I told her. "Don't take it personally."

She leapt from my arms onto the window seat, craning her head to find the bird, bumping against the glass. But the crow was gone.

Another Monday yoga class had gone by, sans Jorn and Sebastian. I'd read some of Jorn's stories in *The Independent* and, a few days ago, had seen Sebastian coming out of Northern Lights. It was time to find answers about Tiger Corp.

I grabbed my satchel and drove to the Strawberry B&B, a tidy gray Victorian mansion. As I climbed the steps of the white wraparound porch, I passed a collection of rockers and hanging baskets of petunias and verbena. The moment I opened the door, I was hit by the smell of baking bread, cinnamon, and bacon. I heard the clatter of silverware on fine china and the mumbling of voices. I peeked into the dining room. It was bathed in soft morning light from three stained-glass windows—warm gold, rich rose, sacred blue. It was like eating inside a kaleidoscope. The proprietress, Ellen Lacey, maintains one can never have too much romance at breakfast.

On this May morning, there were two couples and no Sebastian Winter enjoying Ellen's croissants and huge breakfast. I flagged her down as she was pouring coffee, and she placed the coffee pot on a warmer and clattered my way. We stepped out into the foyer.

"I'd like to see Sebastian Winter," I said.

Wiping her hands on the red apron tied around her neck and waist, she said, "He's gone."

"Gone?"

"Checked out yesterday." She motioned for me to follow her into the salon, a room set up to be an inviting escape. Warm colors on the walls, chairs and sofas arranged for cozy conversations, tables by the French windows for card playing or puzzles. As usual, Ellen was tottering about in high heels; she even wore them while she cooked. Today I caught a glimpse of red stilettos with platform soles under her pressed khaki chinos. Her crisp white shirt was rolled up to the elbow. Ellen seated me at one of the salon tables and click-clacked off to the kitchen for a basket of croissants and some tea. She returned and sat down opposite me. We each plucked a warm croissant from the basket, pulled it apart, and sighed with pleasure as the flakes snowed down our shirt fronts.

Ellen, only fifty-six, had been in human resources before taking early retirement, moving to Gabriel's Garden, and buying Doc Hampton's old place. She had once made her living sizing up people. I trusted her opinion.

"What did you think of Sebastian Winter?"

"Polite. Self-contained. Often on the phone. Likes fine food. Generous tipper. He had the maid wrapped around his little finger." She patted her lips with a floral linen napkin without disrupting the red lipstick that matched her shoes and apron. "Enjoys puzzling."

"Puzzling?"

Ellen pointed to the jigsaw puzzle spread out on a table in the corner, a reproduction of Van Gogh's *Café Terrace at Night*. "Mr. Winter often helped me with the puzzle in the evenings. It's a killer. Two thousand pieces. What was I thinking?" She laughed. "We talked about plays and books. A sophisticated man. He was good at the puzzle. Methodical. An eye for patterns. Said he used to do puzzles with his mother."

Working a puzzle was such a homey thing to do—not what I associated with Sebastian Winter at all. But then, Ellen was a smart woman, elegant in manner and looks, easy to be with. A perfect hostess, a pleasant companion. Still, I didn't like knowing about this "normal" side of Sebastian. He was a trickster, and I didn't trust him, even if he did like cats and they liked him.

"Any visitors?" I asked.

"Not that I know of."

I nibbled on my second buttery croissant.

"Wait," she said, her brow wrinkling in thought. She snapped her fingers. "I did see him once with Julia's sister. The blonde."

"Sasha came here?"

Ellen shook her head. "No. I saw them somewhere else. Walking around the lake. Why are you interested?"

"He took some yoga classes. We had a slight disagreement, and I wanted to iron out a few things."

Ellen was sorry she couldn't help me. "But he did leave some stuff behind," she said.

"What?" I asked.

She held up a manicured finger, painted red; grabbed a croissant; and hurried out of the room. I could hear her in her office down the hall. She returned with a handful of papers. She placed them in front of me. "These were all over his room. Doodles. I've been intending to pitch them."

I gingerly moved the papers, placing one next to the other. There were six in all. All drawn on the inn's stationery. And they were all of trees. I squinted at them, leaned closer.

Ellen leaned closer as well. "What do you see?"

My glance swept from one to the other. I traced one tree with my finger. The trunk had an odd shape, the lines of the bark, the shadows. If I softened my focus, I could make out the body of a woman in a yoga pose. Tree Pose.

Sebastian had left these behind on purpose. They felt like a taunt. What was he saying?

"Can I have these?"

Ellen shrugged. "Sure."

I gathered them carefully into a pile and placed them in my satchel.

My next stop was Maple Lane, where Jorn lived in his uncle's old prairie-style bungalow. If I couldn't corner Sebastian and wring the truth about Tiger Corp. out of him, I'd get it out of Jorn. He was surely recovered from the rumble in yoga class. It was time I reminded him we had a partnership.

I climbed the front steps and knocked.

No answer.

I banged harder and shouted, "Jorn?"

The neighbor next door leaned out over his porch, an identical one to Jorn's, and said, "He's gone."

I sighed. What was with everyone today? No one was where they were supposed to be.

I walked to the edge of Jorn's porch so the man and I were facing each other, barely fifteen feet apart. "What do you mean gone?"

"Like with a suitcase, man."

I looked at the guy more closely. He was the typical twenty-something pothead. I had seen a lot of these types in my time. T-shirts always appeared to be just about to slide off their skinny frames. This one had wire-rimmed glasses, long brown hair in need of a trim about three years ago, and a shadow beard. He gave me an innocent smile. I didn't expect him to focus longer than five minutes so I hurried to ask, "You don't happen to have a key to the place, do you?"

"Sure, I do. Peter likes me to water his plants when he's gone."

"He has plants?"

"A cactus. A real cool one."

"Can you let me in? I left something here," I lied.

The man hesitated. Damn, had five minutes passed already? "You, like, his girlfriend?"

"Yoga teacher."

"Ah," he bowed his head over his palms now clasped in prayer. "*Namaste,* yoga chick."

"The key?"

"Right. I gotta water Armadillo anyway."

He disappeared into his house and came loping out two minutes later with a key tied to a hubcap.

"So I don't lose it," he smiled. "I'm Randy, by the way."

"Maya," I said.

"Maya the yoga chick," he rolled the words around in his mouth. The hubcap banged against the door as he fitted the key into the lock and wrestled with it.

Finally, the door popped open. I hesitated. This was my first step into Jorn's sanctuary. When Randy looked at me strangely, I straightened my shoulders and entered as if this were familiar territory.

Snooping in people's houses is like opening a secret door into their personality. I love it. I'm a sucker for a good house tour. Jorn's house was nice smelling and mismatched, just like him. I wandered through a small living room decorated in old floral wallpaper, two new leather Mission chairs with ottomans, and stacks of newspapers: *New York Times, Wall Street Journal,* the *Star Tribune.* On the fireplace mantel was a red sock and an empty beer glass. The bookshelves that framed the fireplace were packed so tight it was a wonder any volume could breathe. If you pulled out one, you'd get five others, whether you wanted them or not. Nothing but nonfiction.

I walked from living room into the dining room, which apparently Jorn used for writing, not eating. No dining room table. Just a large sloppy desk and rows of file cabinets. I leaned over the desk, afraid to touch anything. There was no computer so he'd taken his laptop.

I heard Randy in the kitchen and followed his voice. "Hey, Armadillo. How's it hangin'?"

The kitchen was small and much neater than the other

rooms. It had a breakfast nook the size of a cubbyhole. Armadillo was a zebra cactus no bigger than my fist, a dark green succulent with white dots in ridges that resembled the stripes on a zebra. Randy was holding it under the faucet and flooding the pot.

"I think Armadillo's good," I said.

"Yeah?"

I nodded. "You give a cactus too much water and it'll explode."

Randy shut off the water. "No shit?"

"They *are* desert lovers."

"So true," Randy said, carefully placing Armadillo back on the kitchen windowsill. He ran his finger along one nubby leaf, a gesture of good-bye I bet he did every time he came over to drown Armadillo.

Before we left, I took a spin through the two upstairs bedrooms. One was filled with moving boxes, still packed even though Jorn had been in town for months now. The other, where Jorn apparently slept, was a surprise. The only furniture in the hideous pink-painted room was a huge ornately carved sleigh bed. This confirmed my belief that Jorn was oblivious to color but could be saved. The bed was beautiful and covered with an embroidered counterpane in a moody shade of gray-green. It was gorgeous, and I coveted it on the spot. I ran my hand over the lush bedspread on the way to the closet. I pulled the double doors open with a flourish, and the smile dropped from my face.

The closet was empty.

CHAPTER 20

RETURN TO HOME

WHEN NOT ONE BUT two men leave you in the same week, it's time to get out of town. You buy a ticket on a night flight to Santa Fe; toss hiking boots, jeans, and a fleece in a duffel; and send an e-mail to all your students canceling classes. You arrange for Sadie to visit a lonely, complaining Bella. You call Nico and book a space on his couch. Finally, you endure your angry sister's crazy driving to the airport in Minneapolis.

"This is nuts," said Heart, cutting off a semi and ignoring the blare of the horn. "You shouldn't go to the scene of the crime. Someone could be waiting for you there."

And someone was.

TUM LIVED IN THE mountains outside Taos at the end of a network of narrow gravel roads so winding and steep they made the four-wheel drive whine. I parked halfway up Tum's mountain and hiked the rest of the way on the path through the woods. A slow march, up and up, memories of Tum playing a dirge in my head. For a while, a young deer kept me company, a procession, like New Orleans mourners without the jazz. The closer I came to the top, the slower my step. I did not want to say good-bye.

As I rounded the bend of pine trees, I saw them. A murder of crows perched on the rim of the circular kiva. I was not expecting to meet the grief of nature here. I had heard of mourning elephants in Africa traveling for days to reach the home of their one-time human protector. They remembered and came to say farewell. Did crows do the same thing? Had these birds been here all this time? It was May; Tum died in February. Or maybe they came in waves. I had an image: word of Tum's demise passing from one winged messenger to another across the land, of birds making the trip according to their own rhythm but making it nonetheless.

The scent of pine hovered like a cloud. The mountain welcomed me, and I experienced the first sense of peace in several days. The stone of the kiva was golden in the morning light, the curved walls casting ever-changing shadows on the stone bench that ran the circumference of the round room. If I climbed down the rough log ladder and stood in the center of the chamber, which was open to the sky and resembled a stone basement without a house, my head would just barely come to the top ledge of the kiva where the birds sat quietly watching me.

"They won't let you near that hole," said a voice. I spun and saw Jorn limping out of a nearby stand of trees with a pack strapped to his back, scuffed hiking boots kicking up dust, one shoelace untied. He hadn't shaved in a while, and there were bags under his eyes. He swiped a frayed ball cap from his head and brushed his brow with his sleeve.

"What are *you* doing here?" I asked, crossing my arms over my chest.

"Probably the same thing you are," he said drawing closer.

"I doubt it," I said. He was here investigating a murder, chasing a story; I was here to say so long to a friend. And now he had bulldozed right into the middle of everything. I liked it better when he was missing. And so did the birds. The appearance of Jorn sent them into a tizzy, cawing and screaming and chortling. They fluttered and lifted into the air but never strayed far from the kiva.

Remembering Jorn's empty closet and how the sight of those dangling hangers felt like a punch to the gut, I said, "I thought you'd gone. You took all your clothes."

"I don't have many clothes—wait, how do you know?"

"The door was open," I said, refusing to feel guilty. We were supposed to be partners in this investigation, after all.

"You browbeat Randy into letting you in."

I dropped my hands to my hips and lifted my chin. "I do not browbeat."

"You threw me out of class."

"One class. I kicked you out of *one* class," I said. "That didn't mean leave town."

"I like to check out stories in person."

"This isn't a story."

151

"We're running down facts. That's what I do. I'm good at it."

"Then why do you look like you spent the night fighting this mountain?"

"Because I did."

"What?"

Jorn refused to meet my eyes. He mumbled, "I got lost."

To keep from smiling, I turned back toward the kiva. "By the way, Randy's going to kill your cactus."

"It's unkillable. I've tried."

The crows watched us. As Jorn stepped up beside me, they started squawking again, sending out alarms to the woods. There must have been about thirty, and more were joining them. The closer we got, the more anxious they became.

"Be ready to run if they go Hitchcock on us," Jorn advised.

Several flexed their wings and jabbed their heads in our direction. Then a breeze swept between us and the birds, like a calming hand. Fear left the mountaintop. The birds quieted, and my heart settled.

"This is Tum's kiva," I said softly. "It is a sacred place of meditation and communion with Spirit."

"Tum's spirit?" Jorn asked, lowering his voice as well.

"Could be," I said. "But mostly THE Spirit."

"Ah, the Big Kahuna." Jorn nodded.

God, Spirit, the Big Kahuna. To those who required proof of life, these were difficult concepts to accept. I wondered, had Jorn ever prayed, even when he was facing death in Afghanistan? I somehow doubted it. Jorn did not believe in miracles.

"Tum built it. Here is where he prayed," I said. "Here he became One."

Jorn wasn't touching that.

I decided not to enter the kiva and disturb the birds any further. I bowed my head to them and began backing away. Jorn followed my direction, and we turned to the remains of Tum's house. I couldn't look at it yet. So I walked to the edge of Tum's world and looked out.

May in New Mexico was comfortable, a time before the heat ravaged the land and the people, making us feel as if we were caught, baked and bleached, in a Georgia O'Keeffe painting. I was raised on the other side of this mountain, not far from D.H. Lawrence's ranch, where O'Keeffe once lounged back on a bench like a schoolgirl and stared up into the canopy of a large pine tree, her mind filling with shapes and ideas.

From Tum's doorstep the woods rippled down the mountain, a living blanket of bristles over the Sangre de Cristo range. I realized I missed these high desert altitudes, the dry air, the endless sky. Even when it was hot enough to curl your edges, you could breathe here—unlike a sticky ninety-five-degree summer day in Minnesota.

Another breeze lifted up from the valley below, reminding me there was much still to be done. Long good-byes were not Tum's thing. I turned and faced the burned-out structure. The home of James Tumblethorne. The roof was gone, and the fire-eaten walls stood tired and lonely. The air still smelled like smoke. I walked closer and stepped carefully through the scorched door frame. The breath was sucked from me, as if I were standing in the heat of a furnace, only it was the heat of violence. Suffering. Anger. Death. The energies were painful. I had never felt such residual energies so strongly. I grabbed the door frame to steady myself and felt a hand on my arm, Jorn's. When I glanced back at him, he appeared soft and fuzzy. There were tears in my eyes. He said nothing, just stepped closer, his support a shadow behind me.

We were standing in ashes, standing in the whispers of Tum's life, maybe even Tum himself. I took a shaky breath, and in my head, I heard him, "Kid, even when you think I'm gone, I won't be gone."

Somehow Jorn sensed I needed to talk about Tum. "Tell me about him," he said.

I thought for a moment. "He baked bread. He said yeast taught patience. He devoured mysteries as if they were doughnuts, gritty stuff, hard-boiled Dashiell Hammett stories he got at the used bookstore in Taos. He didn't un-derstand art. I would take him to museums, and he would shake his head, saying over and over, 'I don't get it.'

"He was drawn to my mother's calm, as many people are. She insisted on calling him James. He thought my father was crazy. Tum hated computers and don't get him started on Facebook and Twitter."

"Didn't trust social media, huh?" Jorn said, looking around.

"A guy living alone on a mountaintop isn't into 'social.' He always said he'd made enough friends in his lifetime." I drew swirls—like cinnamon spiraling through a loaf of Tum's bread—in the dust on what was left of the kitchen island. "He liked to do Sudokus while he baked. He built this place with his own hands."

"Handy and logical," Jorn said. "Not exactly mystic material."

"He never stopped dressing like a Hell's Angel. Black tees, worn leather vest, heavy boots. He said since he only had black socks and shirts, he never had to worry about matching anything."

"Good idea. Maybe I should try that."

"He enjoyed looking big and scary."

"Was he scary?"

"I never thought so, and after he answered the shamanic call, many people seemed to lose their fear of him. They came to him for healing."

"Like a medicine man."

I smiled at the thought. "There wasn't a drop of native blood in Tum. He said anyone could be called. Some say shamans are 'wounded healers.' They survive, are changed, and, thus, are able to help others change."

We walked through the house, stirring up more gray dust. In the bedroom, Jorn pointed to the charred bed. "The arson investigator I talked to said this was the origin of the fire. A secondary fire was set in the living room near the body."

I glanced at him in surprise. I wasn't ready to think of Tum as a body.

He went on, "The investigator can't explain why the whole place didn't burn down. He said temperatures must have reached more than eleven hundred degrees Fahrenheit. The smoke was reported by a volunteer in a fire tower across the way. By the time firefighters got here, it was just smoldering, no danger of leaping to the surrounding forests. That's the thing—it should have. It was unusually dry up here in February. The whole area was still suffering from last summer's drought. Any spark was dangerous. But this fire put itself out."

We returned to the living room and kitchen. Via the open roof, a large black bird swept into the house, circled the room, and lit on a pile of debris near the remains of Tum's sofa. The bird began pecking at the debris, and soon it was tugging at something shiny buried in the pile. I edged closer and caught a glimpse of silver. I crouched down and gently pulled the object free.

"I know you found it first," I reassured the bird. It was a silver cuff with a turquoise stone in the center. My heart stopped for a moment as I recognized the one piece of jewelry Tum always wore. I dusted it off. I recognized the work, the craftsmanship. Etched in the silver band was a bird, a spiral, a turtle, and a tree. The bird, transcendence, to show man can rise above his circumstances. The spiral, the sun, to remind man he is part of everything. The turtle to bring man good health. The tree to give man everlasting life.

Jorn stepped closer. "It looks perfect," he said, astonished.

"The melting point of silver is just over seventeen hundred degrees," I told him. "Most metals and jewelry can survive the flames of a common house fire."

"How do you know that?"

I gave him a tiny grin and flicked at my earrings—several delicate strands of silver braided into intricate knots. "I have my sources."

I placed the bracelet on the floor and stood up.

"What are you doing?" Jorn asked, puzzled.

The bird pecked at it, looked at me, and cawed loudly. I expected it to snatch the silver bracelet up in its beak and fly away. Crows love shiny things, and it seemed fitting, somehow, that the bird have this special piece of Tum. Instead, it bobbed its head and lifted into the air, its large wings brushing my arm.

Only then did I pick up the bracelet and slide it on. The metal felt warm against my skin. I followed the bird outside. It stroked over the cliff and high into the cloudless sky.

Was that where Spirit lived? Was that where Tum was?

MARCHING DOWN THE MOUNTAIN, my spirits were lighter. In jazz funerals, this is a time of joy when you have said farewell to your loved one and "cut the body loose." It was time to celebrate the life of Tum. As I made my way down the mountain, I felt almost happy, somehow reassured that Tum was in a good place. Jorn would probably say there is no afterlife, no heaven or hell, no place of peace. But I just knew Tum had found it.

As I guided Jorn down the mountain to my rental car, I kept a slow pace. He was favoring his hip, but one glare kept me from offering assistance. He really needed to get back to yoga class, and some reiki wouldn't hurt either. He was in a terrible mood, having spent the night on the mountain. Apparently, he had fallen in the dark and had to sleep curled under a tree because the crows wouldn't let him near the kiva. "What the hell is with the birds around here anyway?" he'd grouched. The only thing he'd had to eat or drink was the little water he'd brought and three candy bars.

When we reached my car, I tossed him a bottle of fresh water and a bag of trail mix. He ripped the bag open with his teeth, downed half the water, and sank into the passenger seat with a sigh. I suggested we come back for his car, which he'd left around the bend and down the road when he couldn't find the drive to Tum's house.

"Let's take a spin over to Whispering Spirit," I said.

He paused, lowering the bag of trail mix. "Where you grew up?"

"Nico said someone had been there asking about Tum. I want to make sure everything is okay."

"How far?"

"An hour by car. Twenty minutes as the crow flies."

"Damn crows," Jorn muttered.

We circled Tum's mountain on a gravel road, dipping into valleys, twisting in and out of forests, finally taking a right off the road onto a drive that Jorn swore wasn't there. Whispering Spirit didn't exactly advertise its location—minimal weed whacking, no mailbox. We nuzzled our way through an overgrown path for about ten minutes, climbing, always climbing, until we burst into a clearing on top of another mountain.

"Christ, what happens if you meet another car on that?" Jorn said, glancing back at the road that was already disappearing, as sentinels of foliage and tree branches snapped back into place. I shrugged. There were occasional pull-offs, if you knew where to find them.

I slowly got out of the car and looked around. In the years since I had left, it hadn't changed a bit. Worn cabins of various colors and sizes nestled around a large log building—the lodge. All gatherings, from meals to meetings, were held in the lodge. I scanned the area to the left of the lodge.

There, two cabins over, was our house—the blue cottage where Evie, Larry, Heart, and I had lived.

Jorn got out to stand beside me. He motioned toward the buildings. "Which was yours?"

"Guess," I said.

He studied the tiny community with a critical eye. "The blue one."

I nodded. The little cabin still had a mess of cables and wires sprouting from its roof, a wild electronic hairdo constructed by Larry.

Jorn took in the lodge, the barn, the gardens, the pen for the sheep. "Did you like growing up here?"

I thought for a moment. Home schooling. A revolving door of parents and adults, some disciplinarians, but mostly huggers, both tree and people huggers. Nature was essential to life in Whispering Spirit, a part of our lessons, our work, our play; a part of our very being. I was born here, in that blue mountain cabin. I carried this place inside me, and I always would.

"It was the best," I told him.

"Maya Bird?" I heard my name, and both Jorn and I turned. There he was. Just as I remembered him.

Before I knew it, I was running into open arms, being lifted and twirled. I knew those arms. I knew this game. I was the airplane, and he was the wind.

"Zeke!" I smiled.

By the time Zeke had put me down, Jorn had approached. I introduced the two. Nodding to Jorn, Zeke held out a hand connected to an arm covered in silver dust. Zeke always did glow.

Soon we were surrounded by people, young and old, familiar faces and new ones, all talking at once, all hugging me. Dogs barked around us, while a cat ignored the ruckus from the lodge porch. I tried to answer the questions about Evie's painting, Larry's computers, and Heart's love life, but they were flying from all directions. Finally, people began to drift off, back to their chores, and we were alone with Zeke and his wife, Marianna. With the easy smile I remember so well and a very pregnant Marianna clinging to his arm, Zeke led the way into the lodge.

Jorn held me back a moment. "Who is this guy?"

"When you were growing up, did you have a friend who meant everything to you?"

"Sure, Bernie Nordebruch. He ate my vegetables in the cafeteria, even though he hated them as much as I did."

"Zeke's my Bernie."

"And the girl?"

Marianna was ten—a year younger than I and four years younger than Zeke—when her family moved from France to Whispering Spirit. "Marianna has never known whether to love me or hate me," I said.

"I like her already."

As we sat at one of the long tables in the large open room, sounds of clattering dishes and dropped pans filtered in from the kitchen. The kitchen at Whispering Spirit was never quiet; feeding twenty to thirty adults and children was a daylong chore. Mid-afternoon sun streaked through the windows and across the huge flagstone fireplace. Marianna disappeared and returned with a tray: glasses of lemonade and bread. Zeke rose, took the tray from her, and settled her into a chair beside him.

Jorn pounced on a slice of sourdough.

As I nibbled on the bread, I complimented Marianna. "Great bread. Tum's recipe?"

Marianna tossed her waist-length brown hair back and decided today she would like me. "Thanks. Yes, it is." She sat close to Zeke. A silver necklace sparkled at her neck, Zeke's work; the design was delicate yet strong with a mix of turquoise and amber stones. The slender French woman wore pregnancy like a beach ball under her lavender T-shirt.

I motioned to her tummy, "Your first?"

She gave me a proud smile. "Third. We have two girls, ages seven and five. Already they are taking to the bread. But I do not think Isabel, the oldest, will have the patience."

"She prefers the finer things in life," Zeke teased his wife.

"You lure her with your silver and gemstones," Marianna said, elbowing him.

I explained to Jorn, "Everyone at Whispering Spirit is an artist. Marianna makes breads and is known for her French pastries. Zeke is a silversmith; he made Tum's cuff."

Jorn's eyes went to the bracelet on my arm.

"And those earrings of yours," Zeke smiled.

I felt Jorn shift his attention from the bracelet to my ears.

"We support the community with our art—weaving, sewing, gardening, painting— usually taking our goods to the marketplace in Taos," Zeke explained. He turned to me. "Larry's been nagging us to sell our products online, too. Our honeys and jams, some of our textiles, my silverwork.

I'm not sure I want to mess with all the order taking and shipping stuff. We do just fine at the marketplace."

"A Whispering Spirit Farm website." I pondered the implications. "Larry just wants an excuse to program something new."

Zeke and I shared a smile. He was three years older than I, but we'd gravitated to each other from the beginning. When I looked at him, I saw the boy who made kites for me out of grocery bags, who carried me home the day I twisted my ankle, who taught me how to pick a lock. Zeke's dad had gone to prison because he practiced that "art" a little too much.

At one time, when we were kids and inseparable, both Zeke and I had thought we would live here together for the rest of our lives. Now, I saw that Zeke was happy, content with his life on this mountain, in this community. He had been meant to stay at Whispering Spirit Farm, and I had been meant to go. Still, I wouldn't be human if I didn't feel a twinge of envy that Marianna was living the life I had assumed would one day be mine.

Jorn cleared his throat and leaned closer to me. I broke eye contact with Zeke and realized both Jorn and Marianna were frowning at us.

Taking a sharp turn off memory lane, I said, "We were just at Tum's place."

"I figured you would come eventually to pay your respects." Zeke took a drink of lemonade and placed the glass gently on the table.

"I also wanted to make sure everyone here was all right."

Zeke stilled. Marianna's hand went protectively to her belly.

Into the silence, Jorn said, "Nico told us you've had some visitors asking questions about Tum."

Marianna and Zeke exchanged glances.

"Two men?" I asked.

"Imbéciles," Marianna said. "They filled the mountain with bad energy."

"Describe them," I said.

Zeke reached for Marianna's hand. "Big but not as big as Nico. Muscular. Blond military cuts. Fancy clothes. Looked like twins. One had a tattoo on his hand."

"You mean identical twins? Brothers?" Jorn asked.

Zeke nodded. "They drove a new Range Rover. And, Maya, they were carrying."

I straightened. To bring a weapon on Whispering Spirit land was verboten. The ban was posted in numerous places. The community leaders had turned Tum away twice before he came back unarmed and ready to join us in peace.

"What did they want?" Jorn asked.

Zeke looked from Jorn to me. "They wanted to know if Tum had left anything here. I told them no. They didn't believe me."

I sensed a new energy in the room, the coldness of fear. Tum, what have we brought down on our friends? "Was anyone hurt?" I whispered.

"They hit my Zeke," Marianna said, her French accent slipping deeper into her voice with her anger. "I got my rolling pin." That I could believe. Marianna never did quite buy in to Whispering Spirit's philosophy of *ahimsa*.

"I'm sorry," I said to both of them, glancing out the window at the prayer flags fluttering in the mountain breeze.

Three strings of colorful flags—some new, some tattered from the elements—stretched like long fingers from a pole in the yard to the roof of the lodge. Traditionally, such flags contain prayers for long life and good fortune. It is a common misconception that these are prayers to the gods. Tibetans believe the prayers are blown by the wind to spread good will to all and, thus, a benefit to all the world. The prayer flags are meant to promote strength and wisdom, compassion and peace. I saw that the flag I'd added to the string just before I left was still there. It was ragged and faded. I wanted to climb up the pole and rip it down. I didn't deserve a prayer flag. I had not brought peace to my friends. I had lured violence here.

I had brought Tum's killers to Whispering Spirit.

"So Marianna fought them off?" I teased, trying to lighten the mood.

Zeke grinned, lifted Marianna's hand to his lips. "She is a firestorm, but I am stronger than I look." I glanced from the face that still appeared boyish at the age of thirty-eight to the concrete muscles in his arms, strength won from years of taming metal.

"And the disturbance drew others," he said, his tone serious again. "We stood together."

"What happened?" I asked, but somehow I knew the answer by the set of Marianna's mouth.

"They took the kitchen apart," Marianna nearly spat the words at me. "Slit open the sacks of flour and rice. They searched our homes."

"They had guns. How did you defend yourselves?" Jorn asked.

Zeke gave Jorn a sage look. "The Whispering Spirit way."

Jorn glanced at me, puzzled.

"With nonviolence," I explained.

Jorn clearly thought this was a nutty response to an armed enemy. "But the women and the children?"

Zeke explained, "We formed a circle around the weak, a shield of our bodies, and let the men search."

I could imagine the people of Whispering Spirit—the women and the men—forming a line of peaceful resistance, protecting the old and the children with their bodies. It was the Whispering Spirit way. This was a community that did more than break bread together and encourage everyone to recycle. It maintained a code of peaceful coexistence and nonviolence. But if Zeke happened to clasp one of his hammers in a confident manner, if Marianna brandished her rolling pin, or some of the others armed themselves with garden tools and sharp axes, the intruders would have no way of knowing that it was all for show, that few if any would fight back.

One of the reasons I no longer fit in here.

"They tore apart the lodge, the barn, our homes," Zeke said, "and then they found The Bank."

"The Bank?" Jorn asked. "You have a bank?"

ZEKE AND MARIANNA LED the way behind the lodge to a small building not much bigger than a typical garden shed. As we crossed the grass to the shed, Zeke explained to Jorn, "No one locks their doors in Whispering Spirit. In fact, there's only one place kept locked here: The Bank."

"It was Larry's idea. The Bank was really an excuse to experiment with security." I shrugged. "But people liked it."

"The Bank is filled with shoeboxes," Zeke said. "Anyone can open an account, even the kids. What you put in your shoebox is your business. Gold coins. Important papers. Pretty rocks. We have only one rule: no live things deposited in The Bank."

We reached The Bank, which had seemed so much bigger in my memory. I said, "Here's where Zeke taught me how to pick a lock."

"Pick a lock?" Jorn frowned.

I nodded. "It was the only place we could practice."

"We hadn't counted on Larry also installing an alarm system," Zeke said with a grin.

I laughed. "The night we broke in we must have woken people three mountains over. It was so loud."

Marianna huffed. "They scared everyone. We thought we were being raided. Papa flushed his entire stash. For nothing."

Zeke and I exchanged grins.

Suddenly, memories were heavy around us, and we grew silent.

I lifted the cheap combination lock. "Looks new."

Zeke nodded, "They destroyed the other one."

"Did the alarm go off when they broke in?" Jorn asked.

Zeke and Marianna looked embarrassed. "It was unplugged," Zeke admitted. "It has a short in it or something. It goes off at all times of the day and night."

I made a mental note to tell Larry to come here and fix it.

"May I?" I asked, motioning to the lock.

"Be my guest," Zeke smiled. "Let's see what you remember." He pulled a thin strip of metal from his pocket and handed it to me. Zeke always kept this shim on him; it had been his father's. I knelt by the combination lock; took a deep, cleansing breath; and gently inserted the shim along the shackle of the lock. I twisted the shim and pushed down at the same time. That did it. I pulled on the U-shaped bar of the lock, and it popped open.

I smiled and stepped into The Bank.

The energy swirling in this small space struck the grin from my face. I gasped and fell back a step.

"Maya?" Jorn and Zeke said.

I could sense *them* here, the same dark energies that had been at Tum's. I could sense their anger and found it feeding my own.

The Bank was a mess. Boxes had been pulled from shelves, flung to the floor, stepped on, ground to pieces. I crouched to examine the shards of a porcelain face. The broken doll stared at me with one blue eye. Someone's collection of bottle caps was strewn across the floor. I nearly stepped on one as I stood up. Carefully, I moved through the destruction: shattered glass from old picture frames; ripped books; a baby's white christening gown, now dirty and torn.

"It's all still fresh," I heard Zeke say behind me. "I'm sure eventually people will come back and straighten their things; put everything right."

I understood. I took a breath and turned. "Tum was murdered, Zeke. Shot in the head. They wanted the Down Dog Diary. That's what they were looking for here."

Zeke took a step back. "The diary?"

"Tum left it to me."

Zeke's eyes widened. "Are those men coming after you next?"

I shook my head. "Someone stole it from me. But you can bet I'm getting it back."

As I passed him, Zeke laid a hand on my arm. In a quiet voice, he said, "Don't go getting into trouble, Maya."

I glanced down at his silver-dusted arm, so strong, so familiar. I remember that arm, the veins, the curve of the muscles, reaching out to me, catching me. I remember the warmth of his hand in my hand, on my shoulder, on my cheek. I remembered these things and realized how easy it is to mistake protection for love.

I walked out of The Bank. Outside stood Marianna, hands protectively folded around her belly. She had refused to enter The Bank. I stopped in front of her.

"Since the men came, our little one can't sleep in her own bed, Maya," Marianna said in a low, fierce voice as Zeke and Jorn locked up The Bank. "You will find them?"

Understanding passed between us.

"I promise."

IT WAS NEARLY DINNERTIME by the time we picked up Jorn's car and he followed me back to Santa Fe. We met up with Nico at his favorite restaurant; polished off more tacos, burritos, and beers than any three humans should have; and then regrouped at his townhouse.

Nico looked like someone who found civilization silly with its barbers and speed limits. But this wild man lived like a well-paid lawyer in an upscale townhouse with sturdy furniture, a kitchen with top-of-the-line gadgets, and a luxurious bath/spa that made me want to plead with him to adopt me. Fresh from a day in court, his suit jacket was unbuttoned, his hair was falling out of his ponytail, and his beard was in need of a trim. The diamond in his left ear twinkled. He was maybe ten years younger than Tum and forty pounds heavier. Where Tum had been your run-of-the-mill bear, Nico was a grizzly. When he propped his boots up on the coffee table, the table groaned.

We were all drinking Coronas: Jorn to numb the pain in his shoulder and hip, me to dull the sense of failure that had descended upon me since leaving Whispering Spirit, and Nico because, well, that was what Nico did. He tipped another Corona down his throat, emptying half of it in one gulp, and said, "It's a damn shame what those guys did at Whispering Spirit. Those are good people."

Hours ago, Zeke had sent me on my way, but not before pulling me into another monster hug and whispering in my ear, "This is not your fault, Maya Bird. Peace."

But it was my fault. Those were my people. No matter that I had left, no matter how much I couldn't stay, they were mine. Now, sitting next to Nico, swallowed by his sofa, I was tired and couldn't see how the pieces would ever fit together.

"We're two steps behind them," I said. "How are we going to catch these guys before more people get hurt?"

Nico patted my shoulder with his big paw, drunken comfort that nearly broke my collarbone. He was thinking of Whispering Spirit and Tum and getting rather maudlin after two buckets full of Coronas. "I was always the angry one, the one ready for action," he said. "I used to make Tum look like the Dalai Lama, and that was before his shaman days. I wouldn't have lasted a minute at Whispering Spirit. But I watched Tum change, stick it out."

"It wasn't easy for him, Nico," I said.

"Leaving the gang life never is. Tum used to tell me that the answers come when we need them. Don't push. Don't grind. Don't bulldoze."

"But you like bulldozing," I said.

He gave me a grin and a shrug.

I passed him another Corona from the bucket by the sofa.

Jorn had been so quiet I thought he'd fallen asleep. But he was reading messages on his phone. Suddenly, he sat up alert, began rummaging through his backpack, and pulled out his laptop. It took him several tries to swipe his finger over the security scanner, but finally, he was in and loading something.

"A source here in Santa Fe has been following a lead for me. He's just gotten his hands on some video footage."

"What kind of footage?"

"The attack on Nico," Jorn said.

Nico shook his head. "I told you, man, I don't have security cams in the alley by my office."

With some difficulty, Jorn lifted himself from the big, overstuffed chair across the room. Everything in this house was Nico size. He knelt by the coffee table and positioned the laptop on the table in front of the gigantic sofa. He tapped on the keyboard.

"It occurred to me that even though you don't have security cameras behind your office, Nico, someone else might have. This is the security footage the day you were attacked.

It's shot from the jewelry store across the street. The camera covers the front of the store and right down your alley to your side door."

Nico dropped his feet from the table and leaned forward. "I'll be damned." He fished in his pocket and pulled out a pair of wire-frame glasses. The glasses looked dainty in his large scarred hands. He stretched them over his ears and studied the video.

We couldn't see the men's faces distinctly, just bodies thrashing around. However, when the men left the alley, they walked straight toward the camera.

I gasped.

"Yup, that's the bastards," Nico said.

Jorn was watching me. "Maya, what's wrong?"

"I've seen one of these men before. In Minneapolis. Arguing with Sasha."

CHAPTER 21

ENERGY CENTRAL

J ORN AND I FLEW home together, dragging our adrenaline-
and Corona-flattened bodies aboard the plane. I tried to
do the crossword in the *New York Times* Jorn bought, but he
kept giving me the answers. Finally, I turned it over to him
and fell asleep. When I awoke, my head was on Jorn's shoulder. I quickly sat up and pushed my hair out of my face.

"You drool," Jorn said

I stopped. "I do not."

"Like a Great Dane." I spotted a teasing grin as he turned
away. In the pocket of the seat in front of us was the crossword puzzle—completed, in ink.

Evie picked us up in Minneapolis wearing paint-splattered
jeans and a man's oversize white shirt. I apologized for dragging her from her studio.

"No worries," she smiled.

I told her about the thugs at Whispering Spirit. "Your father won't like that," she said. "But you're sure everyone is safe now?"

I thought of Marianna's children. They were safe but . . .

We showed Evie the photo from the jewelry store video of the men leaving the alley behind Nico's office. "If you see these guys around Gabriel's Garden, tell me right away, okay?" I was worried about my parents and Heart's family.

"Relax, Maya," Evie said. "You don't have to come running to the rescue. We can take care of ourselves."

I was sitting in the front passenger seat of Evie's hybrid and, unlike when riding with Heart, didn't have to reach for the handhold above the window once. Road rage didn't exist in Evie's universe, and she always found the perfect parking space. Gliding seamlessly between two semis and back into her lane, Evie said, "Do you think Sasha is the one who tried to buy the diary?"

It was certainly possible.

"I'm going to talk to Sasha," I said.

Evie gave me one of those looks I remembered so well from childhood. "Play nice, Maya."

AS I GOT OUT of my car in front of Julia's sleek glass house, I heard a piano. It was her husband, Jean-Luc, stirring soft jazz into the evening air. The spring evenings in Gabriel's Garden continued to grow, creeping toward the summer solstice. I couldn't wait. In all the places I had traveled, I loved summer nights in Minnesota the best. Crickets and birds

singing in the soft light, such evenings were nearly meditative, until the mosquitoes found me.

I followed the fieldstone path to the back of the house,
which looked out upon its own lake. One corner of the
house jutted into the backyard like a modern ark of glass. I
passed in front of the two-story windows of the living room.
Jean-Luc, sitting at a black baby grand with a glass of wine,
waved to me from the bow of the ark. He was a dreamy
man, and I understood perfectly why Julia had fallen for
the French lawyer. I smiled at him and joined Julia on the
patio. On this cool evening, there was a fire in the outdoor
fireplace, which was large enough to roast a boar.

A bottle of white wine and a glass stood on the wicker
table beside Julia. She smiled and motioned me over to the
rattan sofa, and I sank into the plush red cushions. "I'll get
another glass," she said. She knew me so well. When Julia
returned from the house, she poured a glass of Reisling and
handed it to me. For a few moments, we sat there immersed
in Jean-Luc's music and the serenity of the lake.

"Where have you been?" asked Julia, adjusting her silk
pashmina against the cool of the evening.

"I went to New Mexico."

"New Mexico's nice this time of year."

"I went to Tum's place."

Julia's eyes softened. "Are you okay?"

I nodded. The descending sun scattered diamonds across
the water, jewels so bright it almost hurt to look at them.

Julia knew of Tum. When she was researching a biker hero
for one of her books, I'd told her some of Tum's stories from his
days on the road. "Women love men in leather," she'd told me.

We sat in silence, watching a snowy white egret fishing along the edge of the lake. With a deep, happy sigh, Julia said, "Well, it's been fairly quiet around here with Sasha gone."

"She's left?"

Julia shook her head, tendrils of soft brown hair swishing against her cheek. "Not completely. Her things are still here. I think she's taking a short vacation."

Sasha had arrived on her sister's doorstep, unannounced, in March, and here it was May. It seemed like a rather long visit to me. "Is this type of extended stay normal in your family?" I asked Julia.

"Sadly, it is," Julia said. "Honey, I once had an aunt who came to visit for half a year. Aunt Valeria was a poor relation and just made the rounds in the family. We had a big old house. We could forget she was there for days at a time." Once Julia had described her southern home as antebellum anarchy and the perfect playground for seven children descended from passionate Russian émigrés.

"Did you like her?"

"She was interesting, in a carry-a-screwdriver-in-your-purse way. The Danilov family is never boring. Where do you think I get half the characters in my books?"

"Except the heroes," I said. "They are all Jean-Luc."

"We Russians have romance in our soul, but the French . . . they created the word, baked it into a croissant, and served it naked." Julia gave me a knowing grin, then swirled the wine in her glass and stared out at the lake. Sometimes I envied Julia. For all her angst about writing and her occasional homesickness for her mother's blini, she was content with her place in the universe—or she had been before Sasha moved in.

"Do Sasha and Jean-Luc get along?" I asked.

Julia lied to me through gritted teeth, "We are one big happy family, Maya."

I laughed.

Her face dissolved into a sheepish grin. "Sasha likes to flirt. She can't resist trying her tricks. Jean-Luc treats her like a puppy dog. Patting her on the head."

"But still it bugs you."

"There is a reason I refuse to have any of the heroines on my book covers in pink dresses," she said. "I won't give Sasha the satisfaction of thinking she was the model for one of *my* covers. It infuriates her."

The secret revenge of sisters. I understood this. When we were kids and Heart got too bossy, I would sneak into her underwear drawer and mess up all her carefully folded little stacks and rows.

Julia topped off her wine. "Actually, I feel sorry for Sasha. I don't know if she will ever find her Jean-Luc. Her soul mate. All the women in my books find their soul mates."

"Sounds rather sentimental for Sasha," I said.

"Don't kid yourself. Sasha loves being in love. And she truly believes she is. Each time." Julia got a far-off look in her eye.

I cleared my throat. "So what's this vacation about?" I asked.

Julia frowned. "That's it. I haven't a clue. I don't know of any upscale retreats where she's headed."

"Really?"

Julia jumped up and walked into the house. She trailed her fingers along Jean-Luc's shoulders as she passed him, disappeared up the stairs, then came back down with a large sheet of paper. It was a map of Minnesota. When she spread it out on the wicker and glass coffee table in front of us, I saw three large circles in pink ink.

"I found this in her room. She apparently logged her itinerary into her smartphone then tossed this aside. Sasha never likes to appear a tourist. I don't know of any classy pampering places in those areas."

Julia was right. The circled spots were all rural or wilderness areas—one in the west practically hugging the South Dakota border, one in the central part of the state, and one on Lake Superior in the northeast—nothing near a big city. Not one suitable "ladies' day" venue where one could be tormented with mud and seaweed.

"Are you worried about her?" I asked.

"Not really. Sasha can take care of herself." Julia started to refold the map, made a hash of it, and swore in Russian, I think.

The music stopped. We both turned toward the window to see Jean-Luc holding up his empty wineglass with a grin. Julia pushed the crumpled mess of paper into my hands, "Here," then grabbed the bottle of wine and went inside. As Jean-Luc slipped an arm around Julia's waist, I refolded the map and tucked it into my purse.

I LEFT JULIA'S ARK and drove straight to my parents' octagonal house. The energy of both places was similar—calm water energy at Julia's and balanced mountain energy at Evie's. On the way, I called Jorn, told him Sasha had disappeared, and asked him to meet me. I rapped once on my parents' door and walked in. Evie met me in the foyer with a warm hug. Larry came loping down the stairs from his office a few minutes later, just as Jorn arrived. Jorn was dressed like a burglar who had just rolled out of bed: black T-shirt, black jeans, messy hair. Maybe he was adopting Tum's monochromatic fashion philosophy. I eyeballed his feet. One sock purple, one white. He could rob me anytime.

We gathered around the dining room table and spread out Sasha's map. Having been fed for most of my life in a dining hall full of spicy yet musty camp smells, surrounded by the hum of chattering people and scraping chairs, I have grown to love the intimacy of this room in my parents' house. Family meals are cozy and personal here, and when Evie brings out a tray with hot chocolate and homemade shortbread, a feeling of being cared for overtakes me.

"Look at the places circled," I said, reaching for a square of shortbread. "Why would Sasha Danilova mark them?"

Evie immediately saw the problem. "Not Sasha's usual territory."

"Why?" Larry asked.

Larry probably had never even noticed Sasha around town. Unless it has something to do with computer code or an electronic thingamabob, Larry is not observant. He would be unable to describe the chandelier over the table, a charming bit of illumination crafted by one of the Whispering Spirit artists. It would be the same with any object in this house, except for his office. Evie was the nest builder, not Larry.

"Sasha prefers a more civilized lifestyle: designer handbags, fine restaurants, Mercedes mentality," Evie explained. "She's always in pink: from pretty pastels to Pepto-Bismol puke."

"I think I *have* seen her," Larry said with a wrinkle of the nose.

Jorn said, "She scares the hell out of me."

I turned back to the map, my glance rambling down roads, pausing on towns hardly bigger than a pinprick. Something dodged on the edges of memory. What was it? Why was there a familiarity about these locations? What did they have in common?

Evie and Larry got it at the same time. "Vortexes!" they said in unison.

Larry smacked his hand on the table. "She's hunting vortexes."

I shot Jorn a glance. The doors of his open mind were clanging shut.

Evie sank back into her chair, her hands wrapped around the mug of hot chocolate, as if trying to ward off a chill. "But why? Sasha is hardly a spiritual person. She carries a lot of disruptive energy." She turned to me. "Does this have something to do with New Mexico?"

I shrugged. "How could it?"

"Let's go back to this vortex thing," Jorn said.

Larry placed a finger on a spot near the Minnesota-South Dakota border. I could tell he was excited. We'd picked up a scent to this mystery, and his mind was already racing down dark alleys and through foggy nights.

"A vortex is a whirling mass, which draws in whatever's around it," Larry said. "Think of a whirlpool. A tornado. A dust devil."

I tapped the cuff on my arm. "It can be represented as a spiral," I said.

Larry continued, "In this case, what is being drawn in is energy, a spiritual hot spot. We've been to several: Stonehenge, Tulum, Sedona."

"We hit a lot of vortexes when we were kids," I said. "Family vacations. Heart thought they were creepy."

"But Maya loved them." Evie couldn't resist adding, "She *is* a Tulum baby."

"Conceived in a spiritual super-center," Larry said proudly.

Jorn put his mug down with a thump. "Okay, let's pretend there are spiritual vortexes. Why does Sasha want one?"

"For the energy, man," Larry said, leaning forward. "Spiritual vortexes are cross-points between energy fields in the earth's grid system. Intersecting ley lines."

Jorn held up a hand. "What's a ley line?"

Larry tossed a where-has-this-guy-been look at Evie. She patted his hand. "A ley line joins two prominent points in a landscape. Ancient tracks that align places of geographical, historical, or spiritual interest," Larry said. "When ley lines intersect, they create 'hot spots' of energy."

"Hot spots?" Jorn wrinkled his forehead.

"Vortexes produce certain effects: spiritual healing and psychic enhancement," Evie said.

Larry was beginning to enjoy this newbie's initiation to the New Age. "Some even believe they're portals to other realms," he said with the eagerness of a spooky storyteller about to make every kid around the campfire wet his pants.

Jorn dragged his hands down his face. "Are we sitting on a vortex now? Wait. Don't answer that. I don't want to know."

Evie sipped her hot chocolate. "A vortex is like a magnet for energy, Peter. When you visit a vortex, you can feel it. When I'm near one, the hairs on my arm rise. Vortexes are Nature's free adjusters. A vortex can help align your personal vortex, bringing your spiritual properties into balance and harmony. That's why people seek them."

"My personal vortex?" Jorn wasn't having any of it.

"Your chakras," I said.

"I defy you to x-ray my spine and find a single chakra," Jorn said.

"Chakras are mini-vortexes in the human body," I continued, "energy centers that power our life force. In Sanskrit, chakra means 'wheel'. I think Sasha wants energy."

"Energy for what?" I had Jorn's full attention now.

"If those guys killed Tum and she is connected with them, she is connected to the diary."

Jorn nodded. "She probably has it."

"The diary is a spiritual artifact. It belonged to shamans. But, as Evie said, Sasha is not really a spiritual creature."

"She thinks she can get an energy boost from these places to help her find what she is looking for in the diary," Jorn said. "She's smarter than I thought."

Larry was ready to charge out the door. "We can't let this pink chick loose on an unsuspecting population."

"Larry's right, Peter," Evie said. "Even if you don't believe that the diary is special, Sasha does. She's on the hunt for something. What about the people who get in her way?"

"Someone's got to stop her," I said. "That will be my job."

"You're not doing this alone," Jorn said.

There was silence around the table. Evie and Larry exchanged looks. All my life, they have understood me, often before I understood myself. The look said: This is her thing. We can worry, we can help, but we can't interfere.

Larry gave a sharp nod and got back to business. He stretched a flannel-clad arm across the map. "Okay then. I'd start here, at Pipestone, near South Dakota. I haven't a clue if it's energy central for the diary, but it is considered a sacred place by native peoples."

Evie nodded. "There are petroglyphs near Pipestone, art carvings in the stone. Some vortex hunters believe that the spirals drawn by early peoples signified the presence of a vortex."

"Like a billboard. All whackos exit here," Jorn said.

Evie laughed. "True, any *whacko* can claim they've found a vortex. They feel a concentration of energy in a certain area. They see a strange geological formation. They notice animals acting in a particular manner in a particular place. It is subjective."

"And unprovable," Jorn said.

CHAPTER 22

PEACE BE WITH YOU AND PASS THE PIPE

W E FOUND HIM SITTING by the clear waters of Pipe-stone Creek, communing with the tallgrass prairie and a half-eaten peanut butter and jelly sandwich. I apologized for interrupting his lunch, and he said he didn't mind. He introduced himself as Ray Grayfeather, and even though he appeared as old as the blood-red rock around him, his handshake was strong from more than sixty years of swinging a sledgehammer at Pipestone.

Here, native peoples of all tribes have come for centuries to pull the red rock from the earth for their ceremonial pipes. Although it is a national monument now, it is still worked by Native American carvers. Only fifty-six quarrying permits are issued each year at Pipestone, all to native peoples. Ray has one of those permits.

Jorn liked Ray immediately, and the feeling was mutual. I saw Jorn sliding into reporter mode, pulling out his small leather-bound notebook, digging for information just as Ray digs for the sacred stone. Jorn had a way of mirroring the people he was interviewing; when Ray hunkered down and swept his work-creased hand over a carving in the face of a rock, Jorn did the same. It was as if he were trying to experience this place through Ray's eyes, ears, and hands.

"Petroglyphs," Ray said, pointing to the stone art. "Not the best time to see them—noon. It's better when the sun's light slants at the end of the day and the shadows draw around the edges. You come back then."

Jorn nodded.

I followed, silent, as we walked the serene trails of the Pipestone National Monument. The conversations of birds, the wind, the rumble of a waterfall (a rare sight in these flatlands) mixed with the voices of the two men. Both in frayed baseball caps clamping down their longish hair, they were communicating on a level beyond words. This was a different man from Jorn the complainer in yoga class and Jorn the doubter. This Jorn was lighter of spirit, hanging on every word, smiling, connecting. He was curious, intrigued, and utterly charming.

Pausing at Winnewissa Falls, Ray pointed south. "I was born just over that ridge. Mother was Dakota and my father Ojibwe. They started bringing me to the quarry when I was just a baby. While they dug the pipestone, I played in the prairie grasses, pretending to be a great hunter on the trail of the buffalo. When I was old enough, they taught me to carve pipes from the sacred stone."

"How many pipes?"asked Jorn.

"Thousands," Ray laughed. "I quit counting."

"It must be hard work," Jorn said, and from the fascination in his voice, I knew Jorn was imagining what it must feel like to lure the shape of a buffalo from a chunk of rock, an art men like Ray had been practicing for three thousand years.

"Digging the stone, yes; the carving, no. Dreams flow from my fingers." Ray pointed to a white-barked birch on the bank of the creek. "I could carve while napping under that tree."

Jorn laughed, a sound I liked and wanted more of. This was why Peter Jorn had become a truth seeker. He loved people's stories, and to Jorn, everyone had a story.

"Why is the stone red?" Jorn asked.

"It is said that the red stone is the blood of our ancestors, deposited here by a great flood." Ray waved his arm at the red cliffs. "This land was created by my people, and only we work the land, cut out the stone for our pipes. It has always been a place of peace. For thousands of years, this site was used by people of all tribes—even enemies laid down their arms before quarrying side by side. To this day, we only use hand tools in the pipestone quarries."

Hacksaws, hammers, wedges, files, and bars. It takes months of pounding on the hard quartzite to persuade it to give up a seam of catlinite or pipestone. The sacred stone is soft yet durable enough to be used in pipes that deliver the prayers of generations to the Great Spirit.

As a cloud momentarily blocked out the May afternoon

sun, I listened to Ray's wonderful stories, which Jorn drew out of him as if pulling on a string, and began to worry. What had Sasha wanted here in this primal place where land and air and man seemed all wrapped into one? I felt at home here, but Sasha would not. There were places where the earth gave up its serenity, but you had to pay attention, be ready to accept the gift. Sasha preferred her gifts wrapped in glitter and delivered with the snap of a finger.

As we stepped where bison had once lumbered, the big bluestem grass brushing my arm, I asked, "Ray, has a woman been here asking questions? Blonde, petite, about as polite as a rattlesnake."

"The Pink Lady," Ray said immediately. He frowned. "Small in size and small in spirit."

"Was someone with her?"

He shook his head.

"What did you talk about?" Jorn asked.

"She wanted to know about the special energy of Pipestone, wanted me to take her to spots where the energy swirls." Ray motioned with his finger, drawing circles in the air, and rolled his eyes. I relaxed.

"She even offered to pay me," Ray said. That sounded like Sasha. "I told her I could use a new winter coat, but I knew of no such places."

"Did she tell you why she wanted to see those places?" I asked.

"She said she was on a spiritual journey."

"You didn't believe her?"

"Please. My people know about spiritual journeys. We invented them."

After what happened to Nico, I was worried about Ray. So was Jorn. He asked, "Do you think she will be back?"

"Hard as quartzite, that one. Too bright for my eyes." Jorn and Ray exchanged grins, then Ray gave Jorn's shoulder an avuncular pat. "She was not happy when she left. She won't be back. She did not feel the spirit of Pipestone."

By the time we left Pipestone and started the three-and-a-half-hour drive home, clouds had begun to stack up in the sky. I saw Ray waving in the rearview mirror and thought of the story he had told us of a spiritual woman who morphed into a baby white buffalo. But, before she did so, she presented the people with a pipe and said, "When you pray with this pipe, you pray for everything and with everything."

I had felt this on the red stone cliffs of Pipestone. Here I was part of everything. Larry was right; it was a sacred place, maybe even a vortex. I knew Sasha had left here disappointed.

I glanced at Jorn, who was staring out the passenger window, studying the shadows on the flat farmland and the rainbows in the tassels of roadside grasses. The western sun glinted through the car, sparking some copper in his choppy blonde hair and turning him golden. In Jorn's pocket was one of Ray's hand-carved pipes, a small one, a gift that had brought a smile to Jorn's face. I had never seen him like this: at the end of the day, tired, satisfied that he had found the truth.

"Why, Peter Jorn, I think you're actually happy," I said.

He glanced at me, his face reddening. "I liked Ray. He was real. No pretense." Jorn pushed his hair from his eyes. "Man, I love those kinds of stories. You know, he told me . . ."

And for the next hour, Jorn talked and talked and talked. He made me laugh. He seduced me with his eagerness to know everything, to see everything, to touch everything. He told me stories of other people he had met, recounted conversations, did a miserable job of mimicking accents. Ray had turned a key and let out a Jorn I had never seen but always suspected was there.

"Are you going to write Ray Grayfeather's story?" I asked.

Jorn lifted his shoulders. "The writing isn't the important thing."

No, it wouldn't be to a truth seeker and story collector.

"Did you collect stories in Afghanistan?"

I felt the temperature in the car drop.

For a long time, Jorn didn't say anything. In fact, I had given up hope of any further civil conversation. Then Jorn said quietly, "I found nothing but lies in Afghanistan."

CHAPTER 23

WHEN A TREE CALLS FOR HELP

As WE JOINED THE Saturday morning Memorial Day weekend crawl north on I-94, we were probably the only ones with no destination in mind. We only had a spot circled in pink on Sasha's map, somewhere in nowhere central Minnesota. We weren't headed for stale-smelling cabins on clear lakes, at least I didn't think we were. We had nothing in common with the boat-towing, packed-to-the-gills, sweatshirt-wearing families bubbling with excitement, having waited so long for another Minnesota summer to begin.

I drove again because, unlike Jorn's rickety Jeep, my Subaru didn't rattle over every rock and piece of paper we met. When Jorn limped to the car and eased himself into the passenger side, pain lines edging his mouth, I said, "You need to come back to yoga."

"Yoga isn't the solution to everything," he replied, pulling a Pop-Tart from the pocket of his fleece jacket.

I handed him a travel mug.

"Dare I hope?" he asked.

"Caffeine is not good for you," I said.

"Yeah, yeah, yeah," Jorn growled but still took the tea. His hair stuck out as usual, and I wondered if he owned a comb.

The silence that had become de rigueur when traveling with Jorn was shattered as my phone rang. It was a hysterical Sadie. "Maya, come quick!"

"What's wrong, Sadie?"

"It's my tree."

"Oh, no, what's it doing now?"

"It's dying."

"What?"

"You gotta come fix it."

"David can help your tree," I said.

"No, he wants to chop it down." There was a long pause punctuated with sniffles. "Maya, I need *you*."

This kid had been playing the auntie-sucker card since she was an hour old. Don't cry, baby. Auntie is here. I'll always be here. Without even thinking about it, I swerved onto the exit we were just about to pass, turned around, and headed back the way we came.

Jorn sat up. "What the—"

I explained that we had a tree emergency. He couldn't believe it. "Really? We're going back to Gabriel's Garden? What about Sasha?"

"Slight delay. She'll keep."

"Yesterday you were telling me there wasn't a moment to waste and today we have time to play tree doctor?"

"Just eat your Pop-Tart."

As I pulled into the driveway at Heart's house, Sadie came running down the steps. She dragged me out of the car and pulled me toward the black cherry in the front yard, the one that had created a sensation in the town by bursting into spring pink blossoms two months early on a snowy March day. It was May now, when all the other black cherry trees in Minnesota were flowering with new life and energy. The tiny flowers on Sadie's tree were gone. Its leaves were drooping, wilting actually. I'm no botanist, but I knew this couldn't be good. From the looks of a garbage bag by the porch, David had been raking up the leaves as soon as they hit the ground.

"Can you fix it?" Sadie asked anxiously.

"It's a big tree, darling," I said.

Sadie put her hands on her hips and a stubborn look on her face. "I've seen you reiki plants before. You're always saving Mom's."

"Those are houseplants. This is a tree and one big bundle of stress. Sadie, magic takes a lot out of a being."

Jorn snorted behind me.

"Just try," pleaded Sadie with those eyes that always melt me.

There was no choice.

Heart and David joined us. My sister stood on the porch, her body leaning toward her husband. From her expression, I knew she was torn—she instinctively wanted to keep Sadie firmly tethered to the practical ground, but she also harbored some hope that the mystical world that was so strong in me could come forth and lift her child to happiness. "Sadie, Maya is not a miracle worker," she said, but her voice wasn't as firm as usual.

I have been giving reiki to humans, plants, and animals since I was fourteen. I was trained by a reiki master at Whispering Spirit named June, who proclaimed with a smile that I was "a natural."

Reiki is pronounced *ray-key*, and it is gentle, healing energy transmitted through the hands. June called it "love from the universe, shared through the hands." In Japanese, *rei* means spirit, divine, or miraculous. *Ki* means breath, force, or energy. "It's divine breath," June told me in our first training session, "a miraculous energy. Use it with love." And the teenage me did. I gave reiki to everything: the plants in our house (they flourished), Zeke when he twisted his knee, a woman from a nearby farm who suffered from terrible migraines. I learned distance reiki so that I could help Martin, the old arthritic cat at Whispering Spirit; crotchety Martin never held still long enough for a good hands-on reiki session.

Reiki became addictive. I got off on healing.

But no matter how talented, a reiki practitioner cannot start a heart that has stopped or mend a broken bone instantly or save a dying tree. Sure, there are stories of people who have knocked out diseases with reiki, but it has never happened to me. I accepted my limits now and was no longer that teenage girl who was hell-bent on saving the world with the touch of her hands.

So, I didn't hold out much hope for the cherry tree.

But David had planted this tree the day after Sadie was born. It was Sadie's tree.

David caught my eye. "We need to take it out, Maya." He wanted me to turn Sadie down, not build up his little girl's hopes. He nodded toward the tree's miserable leaves. "The black cherry's foliage, especially when the leaves wilt like this, is poisonous. If they fall on the ground and some animal eats them . . . it could kill a kid's dog or cat. Not that one less cat in the neighborhood would be a loss."

"David." Heart elbowed her feline-unfriendly husband.

Sadie protested. "But it's *my* tree."

"Your dad doesn't want to do this either, Sadie, but—" Heart said.

"No." Sadie suddenly wrapped her arms around my middle and whispered, "Please do something."

I looked up into the tree towering above us then back down at my only niece. "Let's give it a try, shall we?" I smiled at Sadie. "You can help. Place your hands here and here." I positioned her hands near mine, flat against the broken, black bark. "Close your eyes," I whispered. "Breathe. Become part of the tree's life. Send love."

As soon as I touched the tree, I felt its pain. It slammed into me like a hockey goon, out of nowhere, full of unchecked power. It was jarring at first, but then I got used to it and began to pick up a faint pulling through my hands, a tiny ribbon of life. The tree was reaching for energy, using me as a pipeline to the universe's life force. In yoga, the life energy all around us is called *prana*. This tree was a *prana* puller.

The pull grew stronger. The tree was eagerly sucking

energy now. I glanced at Sadie. She smiled at me, obviously feeling nothing. I kept the smile on my face as my hands began to burn.

Eventually, Sadie grew tired and bored. She sank to the ground and sat with her back against the tree. Heart joined her. Sadie played with a twig on the ground; she snapped it in two and the scent of almonds spiraled into the air. I listened to mother and daughter talk about school and what color swimsuit Sadie should get this year and how some boy named Aaron was giving her trouble. Reiki does not require meditation or even concentration. I've carried on conversations about the latest movie while practicing reiki.

On and on the cycles of energy ran, climbing, peaking, falling; one wave after another. The tree kept tugging. I was not doing the healing. The tree was seeking balance, self-healing, and I was just the conduit. Energy sparked from the air, raced through me to the tree. It was like holding a live wire.

Finally, after about an hour, I lifted my hands from the tree. Sadie jumped to her feet. "Is it okay?"

"We'll see," I said, exchanging a look with Heart. She shrugged. Neither of us thought the tree would survive. Reiki restores balance, but this tree had exerted so much energy in its unnatural and early flowering. It was one confused and tired tree.

And it was a tree. Period. A big, living thing with a massive, near-death problem. How much help could the Band-Aid of reiki be? I could persuade a philodendron to perk up and reach for the sun, but a thirty-foot tree was another matter.

Sadie gave the tree, then me, a hug and followed her mother into the house. I turned and found Jorn leaning against the Subaru. He'd been waiting all this time. He held out his hand, and I looked at him in surprise. He simply stared at me until I dropped the car keys into his care. Then he opened the passenger door for me.

"You know that tree has a snowball's chance," he said, starting the car. "No matter what hoodoo-voodoo you try." He pointedly looked down to my lap. "No matter what you do to yourself."

I looked down. My aching hands were curled into claws.

CHAPTER 24

THE LLAMA TRAP

W E STARTED OUT AGAIN on Sunday morning, heading north, hunting Sasha and vortexes. We reached Itasca State Park by mid-afternoon. Sitting in the state park restaurant, as the hummingbirds buzzed outside the window and Jorn tapped on his laptop, I was at a loss where to go from here. This was the area Sasha had circled, but for the life of me, I couldn't figure out why. Itasca was a small lake compared to some of Minnesota's other bodies of water. Its claim to fame? The headwaters of the Mississippi. Here a toddler could waddle across the mighty Mississippi River, fall down on her diapered butt with a splash, and pop up gurgling.

I stabbed at my salad, mostly boring iceberg lettuce and a token leaf of spinach. My hands had recovered from the reiki session with Sadie's tree. As the wail of a loon filtered in through the open window, Jorn paused in typing, grabbed his hamburger without looking, and bit off a chunk. Something caught his attention. He leaned closer to the screen, shoveling fries and burger into his mouth like a machine. Suddenly, without looking, he reached for his coffee, the one I had tried to persuade him not to order, and smiled.

"How about that?" he said, spinning the laptop in my direction.

I read: "Meditation walks. Tap your inner power with Betty's llamas at the Pink Panther B&B."

"Sound like Sasha?" he asked.

I smiled. "You're a regular Clouseau."

EVENING WAS GENTLY UPON us as we drove up to the fuchsia front door of the Pink Panther Bed and Breakfast, a white clapboard farmhouse turned into "a spiritual retreat honoring the divine in all creatures, especially llamas," according to the sign by the door. We reached it by heading east out of Itasca, following Highway 200 until we cut south on County Road 4 then turned sharply east again at a wooden llama. We drove for a good fifteen minutes on the winding gravel Panther Road, never meeting a car. Jorn only had to slam on the brakes twice to miss deer looking for dinner.

As we pulled up, I searched the area for llamas, but the enclosure by the barn was empty. Before we could even get our doors open, the porch light sprang on, and Betty herself, I assumed, stepped out on the porch to greet us. With little girl rosy cheeks and a mouth stretched wide with perfect teeth, she tossed her long, reddish blonde braid over her shoulder and yelled, "Welcome."

"I don't think Betty gets much business," Jorn muttered as we unfolded ourselves from the car.

I flashed Betty a smile.

A big-boned Norwegian, Betty was a sequoia of a woman. She herded us inside, through a roomy foyer, and into a parlor. When she joined us, I discovered a man had been trailing behind Betty all along, a small fellow with a round face, slicked back hair, and a pencil thin black mustache.

"I'm Betty, and this is Paul, my husband." She motioned to the man who barely came up to her shoulder. "We own the Pink Panther. Bought it in 1999, lock, stock, and llama." Betty and Paul chuckled to each other. "Thirty-six acres. We were looking for someplace to retire, and this place just spoke to us. It has a good feeling."

We all sat. The furniture was sturdy, Betty-proof, but not ugly. The upholstery was country florals in soothing shades of blues and greens, not a nauseating palette of pinks, I was happy to see. Paul plopped down on the arm of Betty's cushioned chair, which brought his head close to the same height as hers. He slung an arm around her shoulders, barely spanning their width. "Betty's my giantess," said Paul with a swing of the leg and a British accent. "And my name is Paul, so it was like kismet."

"Kismet?" Jorn asked.

"Yes, this land borders the Paul Bunyan National Forest. *Paul* Bunyan, get it? Like me. Big guy, just like my Betty. It was a sign."

"A sign?"

"From the universe," Betty said. "We love signs."

Vortex lovers always do. Paul wagged his head like a bobble-head doll. "We just felt right at home the minute we got out of the car. We hope you did, too."

"I felt a twinge," I said.

Jorn looked at me like I was nuts. Betty and Paul beamed.

I said, "We're interested in your meditation walks. Do you have a lot of people asking about them?"

"We're taking a group out tomorrow morning," Betty said. "Your timing couldn't be more perfect."

"Really," I exchanged a look with Jorn. "I had a friend who was talking about meeting us here. Has she shown up yet?"

Paul frowned. "Golly, no. We have two couples staying with us now, both older, birdwatchers. But we do have a single booked for the walk tomorrow."

"Maybe that's her," I said.

Paul, who seemed eager to please, hopped up, scampered to the desk, and rummaged in the top drawer. He pulled out a spiral-bound appointment book and brought it back. Sitting on the arm of Betty's chair again, he flipped through the pages, stopped, and ran his finger down one page. He scratched his head, then leaned closer to Betty, "Can you make out that name, love?"

"Paul, my doctor has better penmanship than you."

Paul said, "That's a 'z', no an 's'. S-something."

I scooted to the edge of the sofa. "Could it be Sasha?"

"Could be," Paul said, tapping his lips.

WE TOOK THE LAST room in the inn.

Betty apologized as she led us to the third floor, which she called the penthouse. A fancy name for what looked like the attic to me. "Sorry, we've only got the one. It's big, though, a suite really," she reassured us.

Following the lumbering Betty to our "suite," Jorn asked about the name of the B&B. "Paul proposed after a *Pink Panther* movie marathon," Betty sighed. "He tied a big, fake diamond ring on the neck of a little stuffed panther with a note: 'A woman is like an artichoke; you must work hard to get to her heart.' It's a line from the movie. Isn't that romantic? Then he took my hand and said, 'And, love, I am a very hard worker.' I would have squeezed him to pieces if I hadn't feared *really* squeezing him to pieces."

"Sounds like a match made in the movies," I smiled.

Betty stopped, leaned closer, and whispered with a wink, "I've always thought Paul looked like a little David Niven. Can you see the resemblance?"

"Maybe," I said.

Betty showed us into the penthouse with a flourish. Although it *was* the attic, it was actually quite cozy: wood paneled, dormer windows, queen-size bed, sitting area with two over-stuffed chintz chairs and ottomans, and a DVD player with our own personal copy of the complete Pink Panther Film Collection.

After Betty left, Jorn and I stood looking at each other.

"We didn't see this coming," Jorn said, setting down my small duffel bag and his backpack.

"I like places with," I paused, "personality."

"You had to say you felt the vibes, didn't you?" Jorn said, pulling out his computer from his backpack and plopping down in one of the easy chairs.

I crawled into the middle of the bed, folded my legs into lotus position, and waited. Jorn didn't look up from his computer. "So Sasha has the diary," I said. "And she's probably coming here tomorrow."

Jorn stopped typing and focused on me. "She's hoping Betty and Paul can lead her to a vortex, although I still don't see why that's going to help anything. She doesn't believe in vortexes anymore than I do."

"She didn't find what she was looking for in Pipestone. Maybe she's getting desperate. Obviously, she's not getting the information she wants from the diary. That means she can't tap its power."

"If there is power to tap," said Jorn.

"We know Sasha is nuts, and if she's in cahoots with the Evil Twins, she's dangerous. Look what they did to Nico and how they terrorized the people at Whispering Spirit. What if they hurt Betty or Paul?"

"Betty could hold her own against the Twins."

"Jorn. I can't be responsible for bringing the wrath of Sasha and the Twins down on anyone else. This is a sweet place."

"Okay, it's got good vibes, although I'm not saying I feel them." Jorn let his head fall back against the high cushions of the chair. "So we get Sasha away from here and then get the diary back. No confrontation in front of the llamas. No complications."

Our eyes met, and the room fell quiet. Outside, the wind whispered sweet nothings in the pines. I cleared my throat. "What are you researching over there?"

Jorn took a moment to answer. "Llamas."

I laughed.

He said defensively, "Well, I've never been around llamas."

"So what did you find out?"

Jorn woke up his computer and scrolled down. "Hmmm. It says they don't spit. I always thought they spat."

"That's camels, I think."

"They spit at each other to establish hierarchy in the group," Jorn read. "Descriptions range from cuddly to uppity. Pack animals. Woolly. They come from Peru, where they are mountain lion food. They have no defenses, no claws, no fangs, no hard shell, no stinging tails. They basically just run like hell."

"Fluffy pacifists," I said. "I like them already. Betty says they are healing animals."

"Right," said skeptical Jorn.

"And they have a calming effect on people."

"I can't wait."

I pulled out Sasha's map from the satchel that pretty much contained my life and spread it across the bed. The third circle was due east of here on the North Shore of Lake Superior. The North Shore was loaded with beauty: clear, cold waters; deep forests of pine and birch; winding roads that went all the way to Canada. After her stop here, Sasha could be heading to Split Rock Lighthouse, the cliffs of Tettegouche, the Superior National Forest, Gooseberry Falls, or any energy-soaked spot in between.

Gooseberry. That was getting a psychic tingle from me. I asked Jorn to Google Gooseberry.

He did so, but after reading a few moments, he didn't look happy. "Doubt Sasha would go there. It's closed for the next month. Spring floods took out some trails and a bridge. DNR has shut it down while it makes repairs."

"So it's empty." I thought that was the perfect time to nose around a state park, no tourists, just a few Department of Natural Resources workers. "That's where she's going."

"How can you be sure?"

I was silent. We stared at each other.

Jorn shook his head and sighed. "You've got one of those feelings, haven't you? I'm beginning to hate that energy detector of yours."

"So we go to Gooseberry next?" I pressed.

Jorn opened his mouth, probably to make another crack about vortexes and wild goose chases, but was interrupted by the ringing of his cell phone. He scanned the caller ID and answered warily, "Jorn." He listened for a few moments then said, "Will he be all right? You sure? Okay, tell him I'll be there tomorrow." Jorn hung up.

"What's happened?"

"That was Ray Grayfeather's son. Ray's in the hospital."

My hand flew to my throat. "Oh no."

"He was attacked by two guys whose descriptions sound a lot like the Evil Twins. When he refused to take them to his quarry, they beat him up."

"How badly is he hurt?"

"Bruises and a broken arm, but he's spending the night in the hospital. He's an old guy, and the doctors want to make sure everything's okay." Jorn frowned. "Ray insists he needs to see me."

"He can't tell you whatever it is over the phone?"

"No, according to his son."

"What do you think he knows?"

Jorn shrugged. "We'll find out tomorrow."

I shook my head. "You go to Ray. I'll stay here and talk to Sasha."

Jorn snapped his computer shut, rose from the chair, and started to pace. He probably didn't even realize he was limping. "No way. We should stay together. I don't want you meeting up with the Evil Twins."

"We don't have time. We're playing catch up, remember? Don't worry," I said. "I can handle Sasha."

We argued, but I had a lot of stubborn experience standing up to know-it-all Heart and eventually Jorn gave in. "I'll take the car, see Ray, and turn around and come right back. You stay here and wait for me." He paused in his pacing and leveled a stern look at me. "Don't leave with Sasha."

Jorn estimated he'd be back by Monday night at the latest. In one day, he'd be going from the North Woods to the far southwest corner of the state and back, probably more than ten hours round trip.

It was settled that I would take the bed and Jorn would be just fine pushing the two big chairs together. But, he wasn't fine. In the middle of the night, I woke to hear him moaning and whispering in his sleep. I couldn't make out his mumblings. I swept back the covers, tiptoed over to the sitting area, and crouched down beside him. For a long time, I watched over Jorn, and when I couldn't bear to see him like that any longer, I lightly placed my hand on his right hip and felt the warmth begin to radiate. He soon settled. The nightmares lifted, and he stopped fighting for a comfortable position. I crawled back into bed and closed my eyes.

The next morning we were up early and downstairs. Jorn thanked Betty but begged off breakfast due to a "family emergency." As he stepped out the door, he lowered his voice and said to me, "I'll see you tonight. Behave."

I stood at the parlor windows, watching the tail lights of the Subaru disappear down the road. When I looked down, I realized I was standing at a puzzle table, like Ellen's in the Strawberry B&B in Gabriel's Garden. This puzzle was a collage of cats, from panthers and tigers to calico housecats. I picked up a piece but, after several tries, put it back down. I couldn't seem to find the right match.

AFTER BREAKFAST, BETTY TOOK us to meet the llamas. It was me and the Halvorsens—a couple I met over Betty's thick, golden French toast and Paul's homemade maple syrup. Paul, apparently, had been up for hours: grooming the four llamas for the morning meditation walk. He smiled at us and led the llamas by the reins, two in each of his small hands. The animals towered over him.

"Here you are, love," he handed two of the llamas over to Betty. "What we have here is Picasso, Cato, Starlight, and Fred. Now Picasso is the alpha, the leader, the number-one spitter. He keeps all the rest in line, but also protects them, stands guard, sends out the alarm when danger lurks." Picasso was two hundred pounds of llama pride. He stood tall and still, staring off into the distance, regally ignoring us. He was white and painted with brown and black spots like an appaloosa pony. His well-brushed coat was silky to the touch.

Starlight, a lacy gray female, liked to flirt with Paul. She blew against his cheek, which apparently was a llama's version of a kiss. Betty said, for all her flighty nature, Starlight could be quite goal driven. In my mind, I already had her paired with Sasha.

Cato, a warm brown animal with tan streaks, was "sneaky but lovable," according to Paul. "You know, even though Cato the houseboy was always trying to best Detective Clouseau, he also took care of Clouseau. Our Cato is a caregiver, too."

And finally, there was Fred. A solid black llama, he was the follower. "Fred doesn't mind bringing up the rear on the trail or being the last to the barn or the food bowl," Paul said. Fred had no aspirations; he just enjoyed being.

"So, now that you've met our little family," said Betty, holding up Picasso's rope. "Who's going to lead?"

"I am," said a familiar voice behind me.

I inhaled sharply.

Sebastian Winter.

OUR MEDITATION WALK STARTED at the gray barn and continued uphill on a trail lined by long-needled pines. We proceeded in single file: Paul first, then Sebastian with Picasso, followed by me with Cato, and the Halvorsens with Starlight. Betty and Fred, who was loaded down with packs, came last. We did not ride the llamas; we hiked beside them, keeping hold of their long, colorful leads.

I soon learned my llama, Cato, loved to run through the pines. Every so often, Cato tugged on his lead, veered to the side of the trail, and swept his body through the pine branches.

"Hey, Cato, what's with the detours?" I said.

"Cato loves pine baths," Paul explained. "They also like dirt baths. Once we get home, they'll head straight to the dirt piles. Undoing all my bloody grooming."

Sebastian glanced back at me with a smirk. His llama, Picasso, did not deign to bathe in pines. Neither did Starlight. She was all business as well once the hike began. Starlight attacked the familiar trail just like the graying yet spry Halvorsens, who were dressed alike in sage green hiking pants and scuffed boots, binoculars slung around their necks. All three trod with sturdy purpose. Each had a mission: the Halvorsens were heading for the next entry on their bird life list and Starlight had her big brown eyes on lunch.

As we trekked up the hill toward our picnic site, Betty chattered. "Llamas are like dolphins. Mystical, highly intuitive creatures. They are healers. I had a friend who swam with dolphins in Mexico, and it cured her Montezuma's revenge like that." Betty snapped her fingers. "Isn't that so, Paul?"

"Yes, love," Paul said. "Tell them about the bloke with the faulty ticker."

"We met a man who had two heart attacks. Then he started working with llamas and now he's dropped half his heart medications. So if you're in need of healing, this is your lucky day."

Staring at Sebastian's back, my heart yearned to be healed. The anger inside of me was painful and mounting with every step. Sebastian and Sasha were in cahoots. There was no other explanation for why Sebastian was here. If Sebastian was working with Sasha and both were connected to the Evil Twins . . . my mind leapt to a burned-out house in the mountains of New Mexico.

As if on cue, Cato sneaked up and kissed me, a tiny puff of air on the cheek. It stopped me in my tracks. Suddenly, the tension I had felt ever since Sebastian walked up in his expensive leather boots drained from me. It was replaced by a sweet calm. I leaned toward Cato. He obliged with another kiss then dragged me through a pine bath.

We reached a clearing in the woods where Paul and Betty had built a platform with a wooden table and benches, a fire ring on one side, and a hitching post. A nearby brook plunged through the forest, its voice a steady rhythm under the flickering birdsong in the trees.

Betty and Paul tied the llamas to the hitching post. The llamas recognized the place. Picasso stood guard, while Cato and Fred immediately sank to the ground, their long legs tucked under them. Starlight nosed around the panniers on Fred's back. Paul gently but firmly pushed Starlight aside, snatched the panniers, and hauled them to the table, out of Starlight's reach. From the red packs, he pulled out human food, llama food, and water bowls for the llamas.

Betty began passing out bag lunches to us—each containing an avocado sandwich, an apple, a chocolate chip cookie, and a bottle of water. She encouraged us to eat and then spend some time in personal meditation. "This spot is extremely powerful," she said. "Ley lines cross right under us. Let this vortex raise your spiritual energy. Become one with the llamas, the trees, the air, the water."

The Halvorsens inhaled their lunches and wandered off, binoculars at the ready to spot some new bird species with extraordinary vibrational qualities, no doubt. Betty and Paul also disappeared along a path upstream. I settled in one corner of the platform next to the hitching post, crossed my legs in lotus, took a bite of avocado and sprouts, and closed my eyes. As I chewed, I smelled Sebastian sitting down beside me. He reeked of expensive cologne, the kind sold in crystal bottles by clerks in white gloves.

Sebastian rummaged in his lunch sack. "Are you going to eat your cookie?" he asked.

Without opening my eyes, I said, "Yes, every crumb."

Sebastian crunched into his apple and said, "Where's your sidekick?

"He doesn't like llamas," I said. My sandwich and apple were gone. I had hardly tasted them, which infuriated me.

"Probably afraid they'd spit on him," Sebastian said. I ignored him.

Finally, I heard Sebastian crinkling the waxed paper from his sandwich. I sneaked a peek. He tossed the debris including apple core into the lunch bag and took a swig of water. Then he assumed a lotus position, his knee brushing mine, and closed his eyes. It was a perfect lotus, a pose many practitioners never achieved.

I jerked my knee away, pulled the silence around me, and breathed.

But it was impossible to meditate. Sebastian was responsible for the death of my best friend in all the world. I despised him for it. He had been lying from the moment we met. He and his goons had turned my world upside down, and I didn't have a clue how to right it. How could I prove that they murdered Tum? How could I make Sebastian pay? How could I get the diary back?

"You intrigue me, Maya Skye," Sebastian whispered.

I started.

"You see possibilities, and I need someone like that."

I looked him in the eye. "Go to hell."

"Don't be too quick to turn me down."

He was laughing at me. I tried to read the energy in the air around us. There was desire and something else—desperation. I had something Sebastian wanted. "The answer is still no."

"Pity. I thought you'd be smarter than an old man wasting his life baking bread and doing Sudokus."

Shock rippled through me. How dare he taunt me with Tum? I took a deep breath and tried to find my calm center.

"What do you want, Sebastian, that is worth causing so much pain?"

"This *has* been a little messier than I thought it would be," he said. "Sometimes, Gunther and Eric enjoy their jobs too much."

My eyes widened in disbelief.

"You'll have to forgive them. They don't follow the peaceful path." Sebastian was watching me. "They are not like us. We both know it is better to let go. Isn't that the yogi's way?"

"You are asking me to just stand by and do nothing?"

"Isn't that what they taught you in Whispering Spirit? Nice

people, by the way." Sebastian smiled as if we were old friends talking on a park bench. "But let's talk about the diary. I have it; you want it. I might be willing to make a trade."

"A trade?"

He shrugged. "I really want only one thing from the diary."

I looked around. The others were still off exploring, re-charging their energies, and chasing birds. The llamas were in their own serene bubble. And I was chatting with a mur-derer. "What? What do you want?"

"The Tree of Life."

The diary held many secrets—from old family recipes to private confessions to notes about things I never wanted to know about. The shamans had recorded what was important to them personally. And in that stew of ramblings was some-thing Sebastian wanted, some clue to everlasting life.

"The Tree of Life is a myth," I said.

Sebastian's expression was patient. "Many cultures have legends of a sacred tree. Europe, the Balkans, the Near East, India, Africa. Creation myths—all with trees of life."

I knew many of these myths, including the Norse con-cept of a world tree called Yggdrasil, a great ash that nour-ishes gods, humans, and animals. It connects all phases of existence and all living things.

"The book of Genesis," Sebastian continued, "two sacred trees—the Tree of Life and the Tree of Knowledge of Good and Evil. God ordered Adam and Eve not to eat the fruit of either tree. But they had no restraint. They wanted more; we all do. They ate fruit from the Tree of Knowledge and discovered guilt, shame, and sin. God cast them out of the garden before they could eat the fruit of the Tree of Life. It would have made them . . . immortal."

Sebastian wanted to be a god. I should have known. Only the penthouse suite for Sebastian Winter. Tum had died for this?

"You are pathetic," I said.

Sebastian straightened, his chin lifting. "The tree is real, and the diary is the key. I will find it."

"Because you want to live forever."

"Don't we all?" I shook my head in disgust. Sebastian's voice changed. "But it isn't just for me, Maya."

I considered Sebastian. He had lied to me again and again. "What are you saying?"

"It's my mother. Some days she doesn't know me, her own son. Some days when I ask her how she is feeling, she answers, 'Ballet dogs eat nails.'"

The truth, at last. "Alzheimer's?" I asked.

He nodded, his hair swinging against his cheek. "Mother adores fashion, and now she puts her sweaters on backwards. She doesn't comb her own hair for days. But, the cat, she grooms religiously. She has not done a puzzle for three years. Watching her like this is killing me, Maya."

"And you believe the Tree of Life could help her."

"Perhaps it can restore her memory, bring her back to me." Sebastian watched me, and I had the feeling that he was calculating inside his head. How much would it take to gain my sympathies?

"Alzheimer's is not reversible, Sebastian."

Something shifted in the man beside me; his energy changed. "Maya, Alzheimer's can be passed on."

So that was it. Sebastian feared that he had inherited the gene for Alzheimer's, that someday he would no longer be himself. He would lose not only his memory, but all he held dear: his empire, his power, his freedom. To a guy like Sebastian, who trusted no one and whom no one could trust, the prospect of putting himself into the hands of others, of relying on the kindness of strangers and paid lackeys, must be horrifying.

"I'm sorry about your mother, Sebastian. But there are some powers we are not meant to have."

"I don't believe that." From the woods, we could hear the chatter of the Halvorsens returning. "We are given artifacts like the diary to change the world."

"Why do you need me? You have the diary."

"You can get what I need faster. You do want me to stop hurting people, don't you, Maya?"

In that moment, I saw something in Sebastian's dark brown eyes that made my skin crawl. Even though he sat in lotus, his body quiet, the fingers of one hand moved, tapping, tapping. He was assessing me. I felt cornered. I wanted to launch myself at him.

Then the wind combed my hair with gentle fingers, coaxing me back from the dark place in which I had fallen. Little by little, I heard the birds again and the stream and the clacking leaves of the aspens. I still ached to bend Sebastian's bones into pretzels, but I could wait.

On the way back, Cato sensed something was wrong and went out of his way to raise my mood. He snuffled my cheek, rubbed against my shoulder, and pulled me into more pine baths. And two hours later, as we entered the yard of the Pink Panther B&B, I felt as if my feet were barely touching the ground. Thanks to Cato, I was wrapped in a cloak of well-being. It would be my armor as I waited for Jorn to return. I dropped my head against Cato's furry neck and whispered my thanks.

That evening, before dinner, as I worked the cat puzzle, an arm reached over my shoulder and fitted a piece. It was Sebastian. The bird-watching Halvorsens had checked out, and Sebastian had moved in.

Betty entered the room, all smiles, and carrying in her large hands a delicate tray with a china teapot and two dainty cups. "There's nothing like a cup of tea after a long day raising one's vibrations, eh?" she smiled, pouring the tea then hurrying back toward the kitchen when she heard her husband's call.

I waited until Betty was out of hearing. "Don't even think about sitting down. Take your tea someplace else."

"And I had thought we had become friends," Sebastian said, sweeping up another puzzle piece, enclosing it in his fist, and holding both fists out to me with a challenge in his eye.

I gave him a bored look, pretended to tap the right hand, then bypassed it and reached into the breast pocket of his tweed jacket. There was the puzzle piece. I smiled at him and fitted it into the perfect slot: the tip of the tiger's tail. With an indecipherable smile, he took his cup of tea across the room to a comfy lounge chair.

I glanced out the window at the empty road. Where was Jorn? He'd left a message on my phone that he was on his way back, but that had been hours ago.

I worked the puzzle, my ears tuned to the road. As I

finished my tea, I looked over at Sebastian. There was an expectant expression on his face. I blinked. His grin was growing indistinct; his face was softening, blurring.

That was the last thing I remember.

CHAPTER 25

IN NOWHERE

I WOKE TO A BLACK bird tapping at the window. It sounded like an extremely large bird, each click a Tibetan gong in my brain. When I pried my eyes open, I saw the bird was normal size, just determined and frantic. It watched me, head cocked, and tapped. Again and again.

I was in a log cabin in a single bed. It all looked cozy— and wrong. I sat up just as Sebastian Winter thrust open the door and strode into the room. The bird flew off. Sebastian stopped and smiled.

"Ah, you're awake. Excellent," he said. "By the way, Betty and Paul hope you feel better soon."

I felt rotten: thirsty, weak, head throbbing, tongue thick. Rubbing my temples, I whispered, "What did you do to me?"

"Just a bit of sleight of hand while you were puzzling."

"You poisoned my tea."

"Poisoned is rather melodramatic."

"What did you tell Betty and Paul?"

"I told them you were struck down suddenly." He put on a fake look of concern. "Seizure. Apparently, you're prone to them. Who knew?"

"Who, indeed? I suppose you volunteered to rush me to the hospital."

"I'm that kind of guy. I was only too glad to pack your things." He motioned to my duffel and satchel in the corner of the room. "Jorn apparently took everything with him. Not a trusting sort, is he? Betty thinks I'm an angel, by the way, and Paul calls me a 'good bloke'."

"Making friends wherever you go."

He came closer and held out his hands, both fisted, palms down. I winced. I was in no mood for more trickery. "Pick one," he said. "Please."

After a pause, I tapped the right fist. He swept it open. It was empty. Sebastian tut-tutted. "You *are* off your game." He then opened the left hand to reveal two white pills. "For your headache." When I gave him a wary look, he said, "It's just acetaminophen." On the nightstand were three bottles of water. He snatched up one, cracked it open, and handed it to me. I took the pills.

"Where are we?" I polished off the bottled water. Now that I had tasted it, I couldn't get enough of it.

Sebastian passed me the second bottle from the night-stand. "In the middle of nowhere," he said, sitting down on the bed beside me. I wanted to move away but didn't.

With each swallow, I felt myself growing stronger. "What story will Betty and Paul tell Jorn when he gets back?"

"That I whisked you away in a medical emergency." Sebastian was enjoying himself. "Peter will go nuts. First, because you're ill, and, second, because you're with me. He'll call the local hospital, but they won't have heard of you. You were never there. Poor Peter, first he loses Gasquet and now you."

The second bottle of water was finished.

"More?" Sebastian asked with a concerned voice.

I nodded.

As he turned to reach for the last bottle of water, I shoved him back on the bed, using the momentum to launch me across the room. I flew through the open bedroom door, the living room, and kitchen; flung open the front door; and slammed into a wall of Evil Twin. I immediately brought my foot down on his instep, my knee up to his crotch, and, when he was bent over, clocked him with my right elbow. I turned to step around him and met another wall of Evil Twin. Before I could react, this wall lifted his hand and pressed an object against my chest. Pain screeched through me, and I screamed. My muscles locked, and I would have flopped to the floor but rough hands grabbed me, lifted me.

I was thrown into a chair before the cabin's stone hearth. I had never felt such pain; it left me weak and scared. I opened my eyes and concentrated on breathing.

Sitting across from me was Sasha, bundled in a pale pink cashmere cardigan, her black leather-clad legs tucked under her. Her head was tilted, propped in one hand, and she was smiling. It was never good when Sasha smiled.

"You and my sister are such idiots," she said. "I can't believe you fell for that map."

Sebastian entered the room, walked over to the fireplace, and leaned against the mantel. A moose head hung above the fireplace. Maybe it would fall on him. "She's right, you know, I was a little disappointed that all we had to do to get you here was draw you a map."

Thinking of the circles on the map, I said, "You could have been a little more precise."

"I like games," Sebastian said. He also liked to test his opponents, to learn how they would react, to guess their next move. He had been studying me all this time. He knew I would be coming after the diary. He saw me stalking Snowboard Boy, even intercepted me once. He knew I would find out about the Evil Twins, had probably even instructed Sasha to put on that little scene by Mary Tyler Moore. Sasha had been the bait, again and again, and from the smirk on her face, she had enjoyed reeling me in.

I glanced at the black wrought-iron fireplace tools near Sebastian's hip. Maybe I could jump up, grab the poker, and run it through his heart. When my muscles weren't mush. "You didn't have to hurt Ray Grayfeather," I whispered weakly.

"I knew Jorn would hurry to his side. Jorn is such a do-gooder," Sebastian said. "And we needed to lay a juicy trail—first with Sasha and then Gunther and Eric."

"Who cares about that old Indian?" Sasha frowned. "All he wanted to talk about was rocks. Sacred." She snorted. "I didn't see anything special about that place."

"You wouldn't," I muttered. My chest ached, and my muscles twitched.

Sebastian, watching me, said, "Hurts, doesn't it? You'll have to excuse Gunther. He loves his Taser."

That's how they disabled Tum. Having felt the pain spark through my body, the loss of the control of my limbs, I felt a new grief that Tum had suffered that, probably over and over. My insides flared with fresh anger. "You bastard. You killed James Tumblethorne."

"He was an obstacle, and I remove obstacles. Something you should remember, Maya."

Sasha flung her sleek, wavy hair back over her shoulder. "The old hippie should have taken the money. I offered. I tried to play nice. He was as dumb as you are. This all could have been a lot less complicated."

"But, Sasha dear, complicated is fun sometimes," Sebastian said, throwing a grin my way.

"It's time consuming," Sasha pouted.

The smile drifted off Sebastian's face. "That's true."

My strength was coming back and, with it, some of my backbone. So, I was outnumbered and they had stun guns and who knew what other kinds of guns. I was not power-less. Tum had taught me that. I was *never* powerless.

I glanced around the cabin at the unfortunate dead beasts mounted on the log walls, the rugs covering the worn wood floor, the sturdy cabin furniture. The kitchen area looked newly remodeled; I didn't see a block of knives on the counter. Darn. The dining table had benches instead of chairs. Slamming a bench over Gunther's head wasn't likely. Stairs led to a loft area that probably contained more bedrooms. This was an old-style Minnesota family cabin. That meant it was built to last. I would not be hacking my way out of this place.

Were we near a lake? I heard a loon call. Glancing toward the window, I estimated it was late afternoon. What day was it? Tuesday? My last memories were of Monday evening in the salon at the Pink Panther B&B.

At the moment, my only defense was attitude. I turned to Sebastian. "I'm hungry. Does she cook?"

Sasha slammed her booted feet to the ground and started toward me. "I'm not your maid." Sebastian grabbed her arm and pulled her away. She twisted out of his hold. "Just give her to Gunther, Sebastian, and get the information we need. So we can get out of this godforsaken place."

"You have no finesse, Sasha," I said.

"I'll show you finesse!"

Sebastian assessed me for a few seconds then smiled. Without even looking at her, he said, "Sasha, make us some omelets. Surely, you can't screw those up."

"What?" Sasha couldn't believe her ears. "Eric does the cooking."

Sebastian turned his head and said patiently, "Eric is on guard duty."

"She can make her own damn omelets," Sasha said, folding her arms over her well-endowed chest.

"I told you." Tension flashed briefly between the couple. Then Sebastian reached out and gently tucked a lock of Sasha's hair in place. She softened, just a little, then spun away in a sweep of pink and flounced toward the kitchen. She was muttering something in Russian. There followed a banging of cabinets and pans. Plates smacked the counter. Silverware hit with a clatter.

"Lovers' quarrel?" I asked, mockingly.

Sebastian turned toward me, leaned down, and braced his hands on the arms of my chair, imprisoning me. He whispered in my ear, "I know what you're doing."

I didn't flinch. "You're the one who kidnapped me before I got dinner."

CHAPTER 26

ON THE CRAZY TRAIN

A S MEALS WENT, IT left a lot to be desired: no light but fascinating conversation, no edible food. The smell of burnt eggs permeated the cabin, and no one, not even tough Gunther with the skull tattoo, was brave enough to sample the omelets. I was tucked between a sulking Sasha and a silent Sebastian on the bench near the wall. The Twins sat across the table, nearest to the only door, not saying a word, just shoveling in the bacon strips, fruit salad, and coffee. They avoided Sasha's fuming stare. I spotted a yellow egg stain on her cashmere sweater and hid a smile.

After dinner, Eric took one look at a silently pouting Sasha and automatically started on the dishes. Gunther headed back outside with his trusty Taser, I assumed to play watchdog again. Sasha marched up to her room and slammed the door. Sebastian pulled me from the bench and, with a firm hold of my upper arm, hauled me into the living room and shoved me into one of the leather chairs in front of the fireplace.

He plopped down in the chair opposite me, stared at me intently, and then began tapping the fingers of his right hand on the chair. "Maya, I grow weary," he said. "The time for games is over. You're fun to play with, but now we *will* get down to business."

"What business is that, Sebastian?"

"The diary."

I shook my head. "You'll just have to figure it out yourself, Sebastian."

Sebastian raked his hands through his hair. "I have tried to read the diary, Maya. I've had the best translators in the world translate the languages I did not know. Yet, nothing makes sense. Boring to-do lists. Mind-numbing whining. New Age tripe."

I stayed silent.

"There has to be a map or a description in there. The tree. It's in there. I know it." He leaned forward, gripping my knee painfully. "Tell me. What does it mean? How does it work?"

It was fascinating—and satisfying—to watch the great and powerful Sebastian Winter trying to keep his cool. I said, "This must be killing you—to have the shaman's diary and still not have what you want." That was me—poking the rattlesnake in the middle of the trail with a short stick. And the rattlesnake wasted no time in lashing out. Suddenly, Sebastian was up and in my face.

"Do not think I won't kill you, Maya. Slowly. Painfully."

I shoved him away. "When it comes down to it, Sebastian, you're nothing but a bully, and bullies are cowards. Afraid of the monsters under your bed, Sebastian? Don't worry. Soon you'll forget all about them." It was a low blow, one I was more than capable of using, Spirit forgive me.

At the reference to Alzheimer's, Sebastian's hands flashed out and manacled mine. "Eric!" he called. The Evil Twin moved quickly for a man of his size; before I knew it, Eric had snapped a plastic restraint on my wrists. Sebastian instructed Eric to relieve Gunther. "Tell him to bring his Taser."

My heart skipped a beat. Memories of that pain shook me to my core. Shock must have shown in my eyes because Sebastian said, "You're not going to like this, Maya."

"Then don't do it," I whispered.

Gunther joined us and got out his Taser. Both men loomed over me.

Preparing myself for the shock of Gunther's Taser, I dared Sebastian. "At least have the guts to do it yourself. That way, when next we meet, I'll have no qualms about beating you to a bloody pulp."

Sebastian frowned. I was betting he was the type who didn't like to mess up his rich clothes or get his manicured fingers dirty. "Gunther," he commanded and thrust out his hand. Gunther handed him the Taser.

Our eyes locked. "Don't think I won't do this, Maya," he warned, giving me one last chance to give in and throw myself on his mercy.

I called his bluff. "Do it," I said.

And damned if he didn't.

Electricity ripped through my body, frying nerve endings. I screamed and bit my tongue. It was probably only seconds, but the pain seemed to go on forever. I automatically began chanting inside, *Om shanti shanti shanti.* Peace, peace, peace.

When the jolt finally stopped, my muscles slowly unclenched and a tidal wave of weariness swept over me. From far, far away, I heard a voice say, "You have to give her a good, long zap, boss."

"Shut up," Sebastian snapped.

I opened my eyes, slowly lifted my bound hands, and wiped away the blood from the corner of my mouth. I had underestimated Sebastian's ruthlessness and desperation.

I have never been so afraid in my life. I was in an isolated cabin in the middle of nowhere, tied, weak, completely at the mercy of men who enjoyed violence. Or, in the case of Sebastian, if he didn't exactly enjoy it, he was willing to use it to get what he wanted. My mind raced for escape. I began to breathe too fast.

Maya, I told myself, *you're panicking.*

Damn right, I am. That fucking hurt.

I think I wet myself.

And now I'm crying, and I DON'T WANT TO CRY.

You are the strong one here.

I am not. I am defenseless. I am alone.

Gandhi was often alone.

Oh, don't bring Gandhi into this and his gentle ways "to shake the world." I HATE that quote.

Why?

Because Evie would always use it when I got in trouble.

She was telling you that you have power.
I have no power. Here. Now.
You have ALL the power.
What do I have?
You have you. And you are the keeper of the diary.

My breathing began to slow and my mind settled. Sebastian needed me. The diary doesn't speak to him. But I sure could. Finally, I lifted my head in defiance and stared Sebastian in the eye. I began to chant again, this time aloud, "*Om shanti shanti shanti. Om shanti shanti shanti.*"

Sebastian stepped back. Gunther was puzzled. "What's she saying, boss?"

Sebastian ignored him.

Om shanti shanti shanti, you bastard.

The shanti mantra, or peace mantra, is a Hindu prayer. In it, we ask for calm and the removal of obstacles on three realms: the divine realm or disturbances we have no control over such as earthquakes; the physical realm or obstacles that come from the world (torturing, power-hungry maniacs fall into that category); and the internal realm or troubles arising from one's own self such as an ego run amok (again see power-hungry maniacs with Tasers). The third shanti is the most important. If the inner realm is not calm, we will never know inner peace.

Sebastian knew this mantra. I could tell by the distress in his eyes. I was invoking protection from him, and he knew it. And on some level, whether he would ever admit it or not, it bothered him.

"You want me to gag her, boss?" Gunther asked.

Sebastian shook his head. He backed away further, still looking at me with intense, searching eyes.

"Boss?"

"Let me think."

I stopped chanting and sighed. "How much longer is this kidnapping going to take? I don't think I left my cat enough food."

That infuriated him.

Sasha had gone upstairs to sulk after dinner. Now, Sebastian called her down.

She clomped down the stairs in her high-heeled boots. "What?" Glancing from me to Sebastian, Sasha noticed my confined situation and brightened.

Sebastian gave Gunther a nod. Just as Sasha reached the bottom of the stairs, Gunther backhanded her hard enough to send her flying. I started out of my chair, but Sebastian knocked me back. Sasha was sprawled on the floor, her hand to her cheek, tears running down her face. "What the hell?" she glared up at Gunther then turned to Sebastian to complain. But what she saw in his face frightened her. "Sebastian?"

Sebastian tossed the Taser to Gunther. He snatched it from the air and took a step toward Sasha. She screamed and began scrambling backwards, away from Gunther.

"Stop it!" I yelled at Gunther. "Stop it!" I turned to Sebastian. He was studying me. "Call him off, Sebastian."

I thought for a moment he was going to ignore me. But then, just as Gunther grabbed Sasha's arm to jerk her to her feet, Sebastian lifted a hand. Gunther stopped. He held a whimpering Sasha like a doll, dangling in the air.

Still matching me stare for stare, Sebastian said, "Gunther, get Sasha an ice bag for her cheek." Gunther dropped Sasha to the floor and walked to the kitchen.

"You will help me, or Gunther will shoot Sasha."

Sasha, still on the floor, squeaked. Gunther crossed the room, handed an ice bag to Sasha, and then stood behind her. He pulled a gun from a holster under his jacket and pointed it at the back of Sasha's head. He grinned at me, and I made a promise that earned me several turns on the Wheel of Life: I was putting Gunther down—for Tum, for me, for the world. I'll take the karmic payback.

Sasha tried to get up, but Gunther's hard hand on her shoulder kept her from rising. "Maya, please . . ."

"I'm beginning to see why Jorn hates you," I said to Sebastian.

THE TROUBLE WITH NEGOTIATING with crazy people is . . . they're crazy. Logic has no seat on the crazy train. Any type of argument is fruitless. Your world-view and theirs aren't even in the same galaxy. In a scary way, Sebastian and I were alike. We both followed the path of yoga and yearned for inner peace, but we let ourselves be diverted down alleys where darkness and violence fed off the rotting stonework like parasites. We were drawn to the dark side.

"Show me the diary," I said.

Sebastian studied me for a moment then snapped his fingers. Gunther climbed the stairs and disappeared into one of the loft bedrooms. While he was gone, Sebastian helped Sasha to her feet and guided her to the chair opposite me.

She sank into it and, with trembling hands, pushed the tangled hair from her eyes. The chair was big enough for a substantial logger and swallowed Sasha, who, without her bluster and spitefulness, was nothing more than a small, frightened woman.

Gunther returned with the diary. Sebastian dropped the book in my lap, but I lifted my hands, refusing to take it. "Remove this," I said.

Sebastian hesitated but motioned for Gunther to release me. A switchblade sprang to life in Gunther's hand, and he cut me loose. He stepped back.

I tossed the plastic restraint to the floor and massaged my wrists. I took my time opening the book, slowly and reverently turning the pages. A symphony of smells— shaving cream, old coffee, skunk, cold air—greeted me.

Sebastian picked up something from my reaction to the book. He edged closer. "What is it?" I looked up and saw a strange fascination in his eyes. I wasn't surprised that Sebastian had no connection to the book. I tilted my head toward Sasha. Sebastian understood that I wanted to speak to him alone. He told Gunther to help Sasha to her room. The woman recoiled when Gunther laid a hand on her arm. I watched the old Sasha slowly return; she insisted on rising of her own accord, swept her still trembling hand down her stained sweater, and tossed the ice bag at Sebastian's feet. She stepped past Gunther. "I can take care of myself," she said.

When Sasha had disappeared behind her bedroom door and Gunther had joined Eric outside, Sebastian turned eagerly to me. "It speaks to you, doesn't it?"

Gently turning the pages, I was overwhelmed with a

sense of home, of being owned and owning. For the first time, I truly knew this was mine now: the dog shit and the lilac, the new car smell and the stench of burned flesh. I was the keeper, not Sebastian. He had no right to the Down Dog Diary or its secrets. I reached one of Tum's pages and the yeasty aroma of beer floated up to me. My heart gave a leap. There, in Tum's magnificent handwriting, was one sentence: *You cannot be found, if you are never lost.*

I knew then that I would deliver the diary from Sebastian. As one who has often chosen the unsure path over the well-marked one, I knew Sebastian simply wasn't spiritually equipped to beat me—he would never allow himself to be lost. But he could hurt many people before this was all over because he believed he could force his way into the diary's secrets. He would not give up. It wasn't enough to get the diary away from Sebastian. I had to stop him.

"I need some time," I said. "Let me reread the diary tonight. Get my bearings." Sebastian was wary. He suspected I was stalling. He wanted me to lead him to the Tree of Life now. "We'll start out in the morning," I promised.

Sebastian clearly didn't trust me. "Eric will be outside your window, and Gunther outside the front door. Don't think you're taking the diary anywhere."

I nodded.

"And, Maya, if you don't give me what I need, I will hunt down Peter Jorn, and the misery he suffered in Afghanistan will feel like paradise compared to what Gunther and Eric will do to him."

Okay. Negotiations had ended, and I needed to get off the crazy train. Maybe Jorn would ride in with the cavalry, but since I was trapped in the middle of who-knows-where, I wasn't holding my breath. I needed to get out of here—on my own.

CHAPTER 27

IF I HAD WINGS

NO SOONER HAD SEBASTIAN clicked the lock on my bedroom door than I was on my knees searching through my satchel and duffel for anything I could use as a lock pick. But Sebastian had confiscated my phone, my toiletry bag, and anything remotely sharp. I couldn't very well pick the lock with a sock.

I sat on the hard floor, cradling the diary to my chest, and talked to Tum. There was a game we played when I was young. It was called the "If I Had" game—if I had three legs, if I had a pony, if I had the strength of an ant. I played it now. "Tum, if I had wings, I'd fly out that tiny window and find Jorn and save the day. And as I was going over, I would shit on Gunther's head." See, that always happens. I start out doing the right thing, and then I stray. The peaceful path would be to let go and not even consider crowning Gunther with crap.

The hours passed. I did not sleep. I explored the room again and again for escape options. Finally, I settled in the middle of the bed with the diary and meditated. When I heard a scratching at the door, I listened for a moment then searched the room for a weapon. No lamp, just a sconce screwed into the wall over the bed. Sometimes efficiency in design is so inconvenient. I silently picked up one of my hiking boots by the bed and tiptoed over to the door. With boot raised above my head and ready to clobber the first person through the door, I placed my ear against the wood and waited.

"Maya?"

It was Sasha.

I lowered the boot and crouched beside the keyhole. "What do you want?"

"What do you think?"

I leaned back. "You're helping me?"

"I'm the one getting shot in the morning if you don't take us to that fucking tree. I'm not hanging around for that."

"Do you have a key?"

"Do I have to do everything? I've already drugged Sebastian and the Twins. Can't you get out from the inside?"

"I need some hairpins and a nail file."

It took Sasha a long time to find two objects that were no doubt standard equipment in her cosmetic arsenal. Finally, a metal nail file and two hair pins appeared under the door. I snatched them up, crouched by the lock again, and went to work. It took a few tries, but I eventually got the door open.

When I opened it, Sasha was waiting, all in leather, from her jacket to the tote bag slung on her shoulder. She carried her high-heel boots in one hand.

I hesitated. "How do I know I can trust you? This could be another trick like the map."

"You want to escape or not?"

If it was a trap, it was a new trap, and I was ready for a change of scene. I pulled on my boots and jacket, stuffed the diary in my satchel, and followed Sasha quietly out of the cabin. On the front porch, we passed Gunther snoring in an Adirondack chair.

Once off the porch, Sasha pulled on her boots. We ran past Sebastian's Hummer and down the lane to a clearing on the side of the road, where another car was hidden, a big black SUV with tinted windows. "Gunther's," she explained, dangling the keys and getting into the driver's side. The car had been backed in and pointed down the lane. Perfect for a quick getaway. "We'll coast to the road. Can't risk waking anyone."

Before I could vote on this plan, Sasha threw the behemoth into neutral and began guiding it down the narrow path, threading the pine trees. I hurriedly snapped on my shoulder harness and scrunched my eyes closed. I didn't want to see the tree coming at us when we crashed. When we got close to the paved road, she started the engine then waited.

"Which way?" she asked.

I opened my eyes. "Way?"

"To the Tree of Life. I didn't spring you for nothing."

"You're going to double-cross Sebastian."

"Why not? He was going to feed me to Gunther. I'm

taking the high road here. I could have brained him with a teapot in his sleep." There was one thing dependable about Sasha. You always knew what team she was on: hers.

"Why did you ever get mixed up with him, Sasha?"

She turned away and stared out the window. After a long pause, she said, "Don't expect me to pour my heart out to you, Maya. I am not my sister."

I suspected that Sasha had figured Sebastian for rich husband number four. She had fallen for him. She was still that little girl listening to her sister weave love stories and searching for her own. Sasha lifted a hand as if to wipe away a tear but then dropped it.

"I'm sorry he hurt you," I said.

Sasha shrugged off my sympathy, lifted her chin, and said, "So, which way?"

It was dark, about three in the morning. I told her to head east and give me her cell phone. I called Jorn. He answered with the wariness provoked by calls in the middle of the night from strange numbers. "Jorn."

"It's me."

There was big sigh on the other end of the line. "Are you okay?"

"I'm fine."

"Where are you?"

"I'm with Sasha." A curse rumbled through the phone. "She helped me escape Sebastian. And, Jorn, I have the diary."

"I'm coming for you."

"No, I'll meet you. Remember our original plan?"

"Gooseberry? Where do you think I've been for the last

day and a half? After I checked the hospitals, I didn't know where else to go. Gooseberry's closed, and the rangers keep chasing me out of the parking lot."

"Stay there."

"I'll wait for you." There was a pause. "I hope you know what you're doing."

After hanging up, I turned to Sasha. "I'll take you to the tree."

"Where is it?" Sasha's eyes gleamed in the dashboard lights.

I shook my head. "Pull over. I'm driving."

"Why?" When I just looked at her, she threw up her hands. "All right. You really ought to work on your trust issues, Maya."

I kept Sasha's phone, slid into the driver's seat, and waited for Sasha to circle the car, climb in, and buckle up. "Take a nap. You have time."

At first, Sasha tried to stay awake and watch the roads, but I took one back road after another. Sometimes I got lost myself, but then I would find a marker or road sign that I remembered from the map. Eventually, Sasha fell asleep. I drove into the quiet, into the lightening sky in the east, making my way to Jorn.

WE ENTERED THE PARKING lot of Gooseberry Falls State Park just as the sun was beginning to rise from Lake Superior. I knew this park well. I'd hiked along its five waterfalls, followed the Gooseberry River to Lake Superior. Once, gigantic white pines had covered the area. Then the loggers came, leaving stumps where once green spires reached to the sky. During the recent spring floods, wild brown water had raced down Gooseberry's concrete and rock stairs along the three-hundred-foot-long stone retaining wall. Repairs were needed. And so, today, on one of the final days in May when the park should be ringing with the clicking of tourists' cameras and the laughter of children slipping on the rocks, there was silence.

I pulled in beside the Subaru and saw Jorn hunched in the driver's seat. He woke with a start and was out of the car in an instant. Sasha sat up, yawned, and asked, "Are we there?"

Jorn flung open the door on my side then stopped. He didn't reach for me. He just took me in with his eyes. I gave him a tentative smile. With a nod, he relaxed.

"What are we going to do with her?" he pointed at Sasha.

"She's taking me to the tree, moron," Sasha said, lifting her hair from her bruised face, straightening her clothes. "We have a deal, Maya."

"The tree?" Jorn asked.

"Sebastian and Sasha are seeking the Tree of Life."

"*The* Tree of Life?" Jorn rolled his eyes. "Give me a break."

Sasha scrambled out of her seat, strode around the car, and faced Jorn. "It's real."

"Is not," Jorn replied, scorn in his voice.

"Is too."

"Who says?"

"I say." Sasha fumbled with something in her pocket. "And since I'm the one with the gun, I'm the boss."

I slowly got out of the car and stood next to Jorn. Damn. She did have a gun, and it was pointed at us. I didn't know anything about guns so I had no idea what kind it was, how big a hole it could make in us, if the safety was on or not. "Where did you get that, Sasha?"

"I took it off Gunther while he was sleeping."

"Give it to me." Jorn stepped toward her.

"No!"

He stopped.

I put my hands up to placate our deranged Barbie. "Do you know how to use that?"

"How hard can it be?"

Make that Deranged and Untrained Barbie. Jorn took a step back and slightly in front of me.

"Okay, okay. I'll take you to the tree, just don't hurt anyone. Let me get the diary from my bag."

Sasha considered us for a moment then nodded. I reached into the SUV, rummaged in my satchel, and pulled out the diary. I clutched it to my chest and sent a prayer to Spirit: *Lead me to the biggest white pine in this whole place.* If there was one still left. I had to make this look good for Sasha. Then I turned down the sidewalk toward the closed log-and-stone visitor center.

Passing the center, I took the path toward the Upper Falls. Jorn fell in beside me, and Sasha brought up the rear.

Jorn mumbled, "You got a plan?"

"To lose Lunatic Barbie?"

He nodded.

"Still thinking here."

"Think faster."

I saw a crow in a pine up ahead. It flew ahead of us, swinging from one tree to another, down the path.

"How's Ray?" I asked, keeping the crow in sight.

"He'll live."

"You don't sound too happy about it."

"He dragged me all the way there to give me this." Jorn pulled something from the pocket of his denim shirt. It was a small red stone carving of a turtle. "Ray was adamant: 'the Spirit' said I had to have this. I couldn't get much else out of him. He was pumped full of painkillers."

"He probably needed the turtle more than you," I said.

"Why?"

"In Native American culture, the turtle is sacred. It represents Mother Earth and signifies good health and long life."

"With Armed and Deluded back there, we might need this," Jorn said, shoving the pipestone turtle back into his breast pocket.

We were about to step off the paved path and onto the rocky trail when we heard running footsteps behind us. All three of us whirled around. Sebastian and the Twins had found us. Jorn stepped closer to me.

"You tricked me again!" I yelled at Sasha.

She appeared bewildered. "No, I didn't. I swear. How did they find us?"

"They must have a tracking device on the car," Jorn said.

"What?" Sasha looked at us with shock. She was terrified. She spun around, lifted the gun, and fired at the approaching men. Click. Click. Click. It was empty. Apparently, they had meant for Sasha to escape with me. Sebastian knew greedy Sasha wouldn't just flee, that she would go after the Tree of Life for herself. And lead them to the prize.

With a scream of rage, Sasha threw the gun at the men and ran past us, tottering on ridiculous, ankle-breaking heels over the rocks and tree roots. Jorn and I tore after her. When Sasha fell, Jorn helped her up. We rounded a bend, momentarily out of sight of our pursuers, and Sasha scurried up an incline and into a small opening in the rock wall rising over us. It was a shallow cave. I started to follow.

"Get your own hole," she growled, pushing back further and further, making herself smaller.

Jorn grabbed my arm, and we ran higher. Above us the giant Highway 61 bridge loomed. I passed under it, dodging around trees, scrambling over the rocks, and turned toward the small footbridge and the trail that would take us north to the Fifth Falls. Just beyond the footbridge was the Superior Hiking Trail. There was no doubt in my mind we could lose Sebastian and company on the trail. As I crossed the bridge, I realized Jorn wasn't behind me. I stopped, gasping for breath, and turned. He'd halted at the Upper Falls and stood looking at me, a strange expression on his face.

He waved. "Go," he shouted. "I'll hold them off."

"What?" I could see Sebastian and the Twins advancing. They were nearly to the spot where Sasha was hiding. One of the Twins handed Sebastian something shiny, which he stuck in his pocket. Then Sebastian motioned to the side, and the Twins split off. They were looking for Sasha. Sebastian wanted Jorn to himself. He ran toward us.

I started back over the bridge to Jorn. "Come on!" I shouted.

But Jorn shook his head.

Then we heard Sasha scream. Sebastian stopped. All of us turned toward the ruckus below. Down the hill, one of the Twins pulled Sasha, kicking and thrashing, out of her hiding place. She beat at the man's face, Eric, probably. He wrapped

her in a hold that lifted her off the ground. Pinned from behind, Sasha kept kicking out in front of her, stabbing at Gunther with her stiletto boots. Gunther stepped around her and
stunned her. Sasha stiffened then went limp in Eric's arms.

Eric threw Sasha's body over his shoulder and carried her
back in the direction of the car. Gunther followed him.

Sebastian continued toward us, smiling. This showdown
with Jorn had been coming since their tumultuous college
days. Sebastian stopped in front of Jorn.

Jorn said, "You can't really believe this Tree of Life bullshit."

Sebastian laughed. "You know your problem, Peter? No
imagination. Everything has to be black and white for you."

"What about Sasha?" Jorn nodded toward the departing
trio.

Sebastian cast a glance my way. "I understand Superior's
quite cold this time of year."

Apparently, Sasha was headed for a terrible accident. We
heard two cars firing up in the parking lot: one to serve as
Sasha's watery tomb and one to serve as the Twins' getaway
car. I prayed to Spirit: *Help her. Please.*

In moments, the two cars rumbled over the Highway 61
bridge above us. Sebastian shrugged and stepped closer to
Jorn. "Bye-bye, Sasha."

"You bastard," Jorn growled, throwing the first punch.
Sebastian's head snapped back, and he went down. Jorn
shook his bruised hand, then raised both fists in defense near
his chin and rocked back and forth. Sebastian was slow in
coming up, wiping the blood from his mouth with the back
of his hand. He was taking too long. He was planning. I
shouted, "Watch out," but it was too late. Sebastian rose in

a flurry of trained moves, pain whirled out of his hands and feet, all battering Jorn's right side, the side that had been injured in the mountains of Afghanistan.

Jorn blocked, took a hit, blocked again. He moved away, and Sebastian advanced. Jorn landed a punch to Sebastian's solar plexus that both surprised and stunned Sebastian. Jorn bounced away to catch his own breath, tripped, and tumbled down an embankment into the cold Gooseberry River. He pulled himself up, his chest heaving, and stumbled back onto a rocky ledge in the middle of the river. Sebastian leapt across a narrow spot in the river onto the ledge after Jorn, but slipped on the wet rock. He went down on one knee, and Jorn pounced on him.

They rolled over and over. Closer and closer to the edge of the falls. I held my breath. I ran to the river's edge. The rocky island where they battled was only a few feet away from me, but I couldn't figure a way to help Jorn. There was no opening in the jumble of arms and legs.

Jorn seemed to be gaining the upper hand. He was straddling Sebastian and pounding him. Sebastian's hand was trapped under him, tangled in his coat. Out of the corner of his eye, Jorn must have caught a glimpse of me, pacing up and down the riverbank, looking for a way to help. He shouted, "Stay out of this!"

Then the struggling Sebastian went still. His eyes closed, and his bloody head rolled to the side. Jorn stopped and leaned back, breathing heavily. He'd beaten Sebastian. We waited for Sebastian to stir. Nothing. Finally, Jorn turned, gave me a tired grin, and joked, "Didn't want you to mess up your karma."

I started to smile . . .

Then a gunshot echoed off the walls of the surrounding forest.

I looked around to see where it came from.

As I turned back, Jorn dropped face first into the river.

"Jorn!" I screamed.

I hurdled the cold, dark water and landed on the slippery rock beside Jorn's body, which was half in the water and half out. I dragged him onto the rock ledge and rolled him over. His wet face was pale and his eyes closed. Kneeling, I clutched at his clothes, whispered his name over and over. There was so much blood. I pressed my cheek next to his mouth searching for a puff of breath. Nothing. I laid my hand on his chest. I felt no rise and fall. "Don't you dare die on me," I whispered, running my hands over his face.

Sebastian poked me with the gun. "Get up."

I looked up at him, confused, unbelieving. Moments ago, he'd been out cold and now he was standing over a dying Jorn. From this mix of emotions came a flood of rage—at Sebastian, at the diary that started all of this, at my own ineptitude. I rose slowly, and he stepped back, keeping the gun leveled at my chest.

I swept up the diary that I'd dropped beside Jorn and shook it in Sebastian's face. "Is this what you want? Is it? Then go get it!"

I turned around in a circle, my ears filled with the crashing cascade of water, and flung the diary over the falls like a shot putter. For a moment, I thought Sebastian was going to jump in after it.

"Are you mad?" he screamed at me.

The thunder of the falls encased us as we glared at each other. The air around us was electric with fury. I have never wanted to hurt someone so badly. With shock, I realized this feeling inside me was hatred—and I don't do hatred. My upbringing, my yogic beliefs, all screamed against it.

Sebastian stepped back from the edge. I had shaken him. He looked at me as one would any crazy woman—with wariness. He raised the gun again to my chest and said, "Take me to the tree. Now."

I lifted my chin.

And from the corner of my eye, I saw a black blur, swooping toward us; death cawing, crying; sharp beak and diving wings, knocking the gun from Sebastian's hand. He cried out as the gun flew into the water.

I didn't hesitate, didn't think. I whirled and caught his head with a roundhouse kick, knocking him off-balance. My follow-up punch glanced off his shoulder. He backhanded me. I went down, my face on fire. Sebastian kicked me in the ribs, in the thigh, and I rolled away. I staggered to my feet. From the corner of my eye, I saw him slowly advancing. I waited until he was nearly upon me then lashed out with a side kick to his knee.

The moment I connected I knew the knee was gone. I'd caught him just right. I saw him windmill in the air, over the water, a look of surprise on his face.

As suddenly as that, the fighter in me faded and the yogi was back, the one who believed in *ahimsa*, do no harm to any creature. I sprang to catch his hand. But I was too late.

His body spread its wings over the air, and he was swallowed by the mists of the falls. I stared into the churning waters, into the pool below.

Sebastian Winter was gone.

Hugging myself, I limped over to Jorn, lying so still on this rocky island. I collapsed beside him and stroked his face. He felt cold. I couldn't give up on him. I was impulsive, prone to landing in trouble, and probably would never get close to enlightenment, but I wasn't a quitter. I never lost hope. I cleared my mind, took deep breaths, placed my hands over the bullet hole in Jorn's chest. I waited. Nothing.

"Come on," I whispered.

Jorn's body was not drawing energy.

For reiki to help, the recipient had to cooperate, had to want to live. I continued to press, searching for that familiar warming, that tingling of a being still desperate to stay in this world.

Nothing.

I raised my face to the sky and screamed, "Help me!"

I tried to pray to Spirit and Tum, but I couldn't think of the words. The river roared around us. The wind picked up, carrying the fall's mist up and over us. I shivered. And then I felt it. Energy.

Jorn was taking energy.

My hands came alive, *prana* sparking. The wind grew stronger. I held on. My hands were aching. I held on. The pain flashed up my arms, stronger than I had ever known it. I held on.

To Jorn.

CHAPTER 28

HONEST, THAT'S
HOW IT HAPPENED

WITH SASHA'S PHONE, I called nine-one-one. The paramedics came and the sheriff and the park rangers. When they got there, Jorn still hadn't regained consciousness. They took him to the hospital. I didn't get to follow immediately. The sheriff had a notebook full of questions, and he asked every one of them while the rangers and deputies looked for Sebastian's body.

They didn't find it.

Sebastian Winter could have survived the thirty-foot drop over the Upper Falls of Gooseberry. He could have ridden the Gooseberry River like a sled over the Middle and Lower Falls, over sharp rocks and hidden ledges, through deep pools, along the River View Trail, out past Agate Beach, and into the endless cold of Lake Superior. And lived. The sheriff and rangers, however, said it was unlikely. They maintained that, at this very moment, Sebastian's body was probably at the nethermost regions of the largest freshwater lake in the world, making friends with the bottom-feeding carp.

But I wasn't counting on it.

A deputy plucked Sebastian's gun from the shallow waters at the top of the falls. In the end, ballistics would match its bullets to the one in Jorn, and Jorn's own statement would support my wild story.

As the paramedics drove Jorn away to meet a talented surgeon who would dig out the bullet, repair the damage to Jorn's broken body, and exclaim that it was a miracle Jorn was even alive since the bullet nearly nipped the edge of his heart, I searched the shores of Gooseberry River.

I did not find Sebastian Winter either.

As I wandered up and down the riverbanks, the voices of the rescue workers mixed with the rushing sound of the water. They would search for Sebastian until dark, according to the sheriff. If they still hadn't found Sebastian, they would come back tomorrow. I was free to go, the sheriff said.

But I wasn't.

I had left the Down Dog Diary out of my account to the sheriff. With a toothpick in the corner of his mouth and a Minnesota Twins baseball cap pulled low over his neatly trimmed hair, the sheriff didn't look like the type who be-lieved in mythological trees. He had long ago stopped being surprised by life or the stupidity of humans. He was the man you called when a deer leaped through your windshield or your ice house was burning down. I thanked him, turned away from his knowing eyes, and scanned the river. It was calling me. Where was the diary? I had lost it. Again. Just threw it away in a fit of rage. That was what Evie would call "a rash moment." I have learned, on more than one occasion, that rash moments come back to bite you.

Sure, pitching the diary to the depths of Gooseberry River was a crazy thing to do, but it also had been sound strategy. I had reacted without thinking, practicing the lessons of Tum: find a way to throw your opponent off balance. Sebastian had never expected me to destroy the diary.

I looked upriver at the white water spilling down the rocks and tried to gauge where the current would take some traveling item. My eyes followed the river's edges and nooks and crannies. Somehow, I knew the diary was out there, waiting for me. Maybe it would be better if a rescue worker stumbled upon it and tossed it in the trash. Maybe it needed to be buried deep in some rural landfill. It had inspired such heartache, and not just my own. And yet, I couldn't give it up. So I wandered the river, pouncing on every scrap of flotsam riding the rippling current.

The light was leaving and the sheriff department's searchers were packing it in for the day, when I spotted the diary. It was wedged between two round river-smoothed stones. I let out a cry and splashed into the water. The cold current tugged at my knees as I plucked the soggy book from the water and wiped the old leather cover on my jacket. The rubber band had held the pages together, secured tightly. There was a chance the water hadn't crept too deeply into the diary's heart. Maybe when I had dried it out, there would be only a few irreparably faded and rippled pages.

I waded slowly back to shore, sat down on a boulder, and hugged the diary to my chest. I took a deep breath, carefully slipped the rubber band from its place, and opened the diary.

The scent of peace greeted me.

CHAPTER 29

TURTLE WINS, AGAIN

N EAR THE KIVA OF James Tumblethorne, shaman, rises a pine of splendid proportions and grandeur. The light sparkles through its branches, and when I squint my eyes and look into its boughs, I can see *prana*, colorful energy zipping and bouncing around. Now, I am not saying that it is *the* Tree of Life. However, evergreen trees, like Tum's pine, are a symbol of undying life, of immortality. And this tree reaches so high, its limbs plunge into the clouds.

"It is said," I told the bird perched beside me, "that the Tree of Life connects the earth and the heavens, a ladder between worlds."

The crow remained still, which I took to mean it wanted to know more.

"In India, there are stories of the cosmic tree called Asvattha. It is the world spirit. This tree, however, reverses the usual order. Its roots are in the sky, and its branches grow downward to cover the earth."

"Tough tree to climb."

I looked up from my seat inside the kiva and saw Jorn above me, leaning on a cane at the lip of Tum's ceremonial home. He was still pale. Two months ago, he was lying lifeless on a slab of rock. He was supposed to be in bed, back in Minnesota, healing, having his meals nuked and delivered by the guy next door. I'd left a freezer full of soups and pasta dishes. He had no business being in New Mexico.

I was here to meditate. The events of Gooseberry Falls still haunted me. Every day with every atom of my being, I yearned for inner peace, and yet I kept hitting these bumps. It wasn't just that I had taken part in the death of Sebastian Winter, but that I had *wanted* it. I had *hungered* for revenge. Patanjali, the father of yoga, would have had something to say about that.

Ever since I had arrived here, the giant pine had been filling with crows. They were curiously silent, watchful. Even Jorn's appearance had not set them off. The large bird beside me unfurled its lustrous ebony wings. Ignoring Jorn, I told the bird, "He's supposed to be recovering, writing stories for his paper or something." The bird cocked its head toward Jorn. I raised my voice. "Not following me around."

Jorn yelled down to us, as if asking permission to come aboard. "Can I come down?"

I eyed the ladder made of thick logs. "I don't know. Can you?"

Jorn mumbled to himself, tossed his cane down, hefted his backpack more securely on his shoulders, then turned around and started backing down the ladder. Watching him, I fingered the pipestone carving in my pocket. The turtle, which I had found lying near Jorn on the wet rock in the middle of the Gooseberry River, had a small chip in it. The bullet from Sebastian's gun had been heading straight for Jorn's heart. Sebastian was an expert marksman, after all. But it was intercepted by this small object, a turtle carved by Ray Grayfeather.

Maybe the turtle saved Jorn. Maybe Spirit protected him. I didn't know, and I didn't care. I was just grateful. But, I didn't tell Jorn that. I rose and picked up Jorn's cane. When he reached the bottom and stepped onto the dirt floor, I handed it to him. Jorn shuffled over and plopped down on the stone seat, frightening the bird away.

"You missed our reiki appointment yesterday," he said.

I joined him on the seat. "So you chased me all the way to New Mexico?"

"Then you left me all alone with Randy and Armadillo."

"Men make such lousy patients."

We exchanged looks and broke into grins.

Before I left, Julia reported that Sasha had surfaced in Monaco, claiming she needed a long vacation on the continent. I did not tell Julia about Sasha's involvement with Sebastian. I imagined the Danilov holiday gatherings were hectic enough without my throwing that little bone of contention into the borscht.

I told Jorn, "I don't know how she did it, but Sasha out-smarted the Evil Twins."

"My cactus can outsmart the Twins," said Jorn.

I laughed. It was July and much warmer than the last time we were in New Mexico. The afternoon sun was beginning to draw shadows on the kiva walls, walls that still held its warmth. Jorn relaxed against them and sighed.

As the day turned soft and pleasant, we sat wrapped in the arms of the holy place that Tum had carved from the earth. It was nice, this nearness of friends, sharing Jorn with the spirit of Tum, as if I were introducing them, at last.

"What did you wish for?" I asked Jorn. "On that day we burned the wishes."

Jorn didn't say anything for so long, I turned to him. He actually looked embarrassed.

"Well," I persisted.

He mumbled something.

I nudged him. "What?"

He let out a sound of resignation. "World peace."

We stared at each other, and then we were laughing.

Jorn unzipped his pack and brought out a Thermos. He took out two tin cups and poured in a greenish liquid. The aroma of mint tea circled us.

"Drove by David's on the way to the airport," Jorn said, handing me a cup. "That tree is gonna make it."

"You had your doubts," I said, sipping the warm drink.

"So did you. Admit it."

I shrugged and closed my eyes.

"Sometimes you are scary, Maya Skye," Jorn said.

I peeked at him and found him staring at me.

"And that bothers you?" I asked. "All that *namaste* crap, as you call it?"

Jorn took his time answering. Out of the peaceful day came a breeze, lifted up from the valley below. It swirled down into the kiva. He shifted, lifted his cup. "I can handle it," he said.

So, Jorn and I weren't finished with each other yet. That made me happy.

Suddenly, the silence of the crows ended. They sprang from the branches of the tree in a clamor of black wings and laughing cries.

One circled above us several times, cawed, then followed the others.

THE DOWN DOG DIARY has disappeared again.

I gave it to Larry, who is good at making things vanish. Before Larry spirited the diary away, I made a new entry. My first. As the fragrance of apples lifted from the page, I wrote:

Gandhi said, "In a gentle way, you can shake the world." But we all can't be Gandhi.

ACKNOWLEDGMENTS

I WOULD LIKE TO THANK those who have so generously given me their time, attention, and wisdom while writing this book: Marlys Dooley, Lois West Duffy, Miriam Karmel, Janet Hanafin, Jean Housh, Ann Woodbeck, and our talented leader, Faith Sullivan. You put up with me, you pull me back from the abyss, and sometimes you give me a nudge over the edge. I am so fortunate to have you.

Thank you also to several mentors and guides: Deb Irestone, founder of Shamans Hearth Spiritual Community of Venus Rising, who enlightened me about the shamanic way; Debbie Gawrych, a loyal reader and inspiring friend; Jillian Pransky, my patient yoga teacher; Richard Pinneau, who trained me in reiki; and Juliet Roberts, one of my loving editors.

My thanks to Kathey Amaral, Cathleen Tarawhiti, and Monique Wanner for collaborating on a stunning cover.

To Suzanne Roberts and Sarah Roberts Delacueva, you are the light in my world. I am eternally grateful for your love, energy, and laughter. Also, a special thanks goes to Sarah for editing this book when it was not particularly convenient for her to do so; I appreciate your observations, catches, and suggestions. Thank you to Brian Peterson-Delacueva for taking care of Sarah (especially when she is editing) and always supporting the family. Finally, and most importantly, thank you to Tony Roberts—you take care of me and never stop believing in me. You inspire me to reach higher, go longer, and never give up. Thank you for always having my back and being my best friend.

ABOUT THE AUTHOR

IN ADDITION TO *Down Dog Diary*, Sherry Roberts is the author of *Book of Mercy*, a funny novel about a serious issue: censorship; *Maud's House*, a story of lost-and-found creativity; and *WriteTips*, a guide to giving your writing power and improving your business. She has contributed essays and articles to national publications such as *USA Today* and anthologies such as the *Saint Paul Almanac*. Her short fiction has been published in newspapers, literary magazines, and *O. Henry Literary Festival Short Stories*.

She lives in Minnesota, where she feeds the hummingbirds in the summer; walks in the snow in the winter; and writes, edits, and designs books as well as websites and business communications for The Roberts Group.

Visit Sherry's website at www.sherry-roberts.com.

WHAT'S NEXT?

SIGN UP FOR SHERRY'S EMAIL LIST (sherry-roberts.com) for updates on future writing—plus get free books, short stories, or other offers available only to fans! Your email will never be shared, you can unsubscribe at any time, and Sherry promises not to paper your inbox with emails.

Also follow Sherry Roberts Author on Facebook to get the latest on her books and writing in general.

LEAVE A REVIEW. If you enjoyed this book, please consider leaving a brief review on Goodreads, Amazon, or other retailer site. Readers spreading the word to other readers is invaluable to authors and their work. If you're shy, just drop me a line on the contact page of sherry-roberts.com. Your support and ideas are important to me. I promise I'll write back.

CHECK OUT MY OTHER BOOKS. In *Warrior's Revenge*, yoga teacher Maya Skye faces an opponent not only bent on revenge—but murder. In *Book of Mercy*, a dyslexic woman takes on a town banning books. In *Maud's House*, an artist loses her creativity but finds love. All of my books are available in paperback and eBook at sherry-roberts.com, Amazon, and other retail outlets. If you can't find my books in your local bookstore, ask for them. Ask your local library to carry my books.

www.ingramcontent.com/pod-product-compliance
Lightning Source LLC
Chambersburg PA
CBHW020743250626
47155CB00003B/891